PERSES

NOMAD SERIES — BOOK 3

K.A.FINN

Also by K.A. Finn

Nomad Series (Space Opera)
Ares
Nemesis
Perses
Chaos
Mania
Cronus
Talos (TBA)

Blackjacks Series (Paranormal Romance)
Breaking Phoenix
Reviving Davyn
Defying Shep (2023)
Unraveling Fallon (TBA)

Broken Chords (Rockstar Romance)
Broken Rock (Tate)
Fractured Rock (Gregg)
Split Rock (Tate – 2023)
Crushed Rock (Luke – TBA)
Shattered Rock (Dillon – TBA)

A bit of a Nomad herself, **K.A. Finn** has wandered around Ireland and the UK for decades before settling back in Ireland with her husband and kids (two and four legged).

Visit K.A. Finn online:

www.kafinn.com
(trailers, excerpts, artwork, playlists etc)

Facebook: kafinnauthor

Instagram: kafinnauthor

Twitter @K_A_Finn

Cover design by Deranged Doctor Design

www.derangeddoctordesign.com

Published by Cooper Publishing

www.cooperbookservices.com

Edited by Desert Mystic Literary Editing

www.desertmysticliteraryediting.com

ISBN: 978-1-914177-32-3

First Edition: January 2017
Second Edition: September 2020

Coming next

MANIA
&
CRONUS

Nomad Series Book 5 & 6

To my family.
Thank you for supporting me when I return to reality

PERSES

NOMAD SERIES – BOOK 3

K.A.FINN

'Never thought I'd have to wear one of these,' Garvan grumbles to himself.

Bray glances over at him, barely managing to hold back a laugh at the sight of the large man struggling to force his thick arms into the tight sleeves of the Foundation uniform. 'It suits you.'

Garvan glares at him before focusing on his task again. 'You just couldn't have found someone the same size as me, could you?'

Bray finishes pulling on his own Foundation issue jacket. 'Slim pickings.'

Garvan grunts. 'Slim is right.'

Bray fastens his borrowed jacket, all too aware

they could have company any minute. As soon as they realised their excursion was going to end in an unplanned holiday on Earth, they set to work erasing any evidence of their presence. The large vessel was quickly gaining ground on Earth leaving little time for the task. They barely had enough time to drag the body of Forty-Three to one of the smaller storage rooms off the main cargo bay before the ship landed. After some desperate searching, Garvan finally found the perfect hiding place. The access tunnels that ran behind the wall panels of the ship would keep the body out of sight until they were far enough away.

'How do I look?' Garvan holds his arms out to the side and spins around. In spite of the seriousness of their predicament, Bray can't help but laugh. How the large ex-prisoner had managed to convince the sleeves of the Foundation jacket to accommodate his arms he'll never know.

'Ridiculous. It'll have to do though.' He takes the cap from the body at his feet and pulls it over his hair to hide his implant. 'Give me a hand with these two.'

Garvan frowns at Bray. 'That supposed to be funny?'

Bray glances at the two severed right hands on the box beside him. He grins and shrugs. 'Bad choice of words. C'mon.'

Garvan takes hold of the feet of the first hand donor while Bray grabs the man under his arms. After a bit of manoeuvring, he joins Forty-Three in the cramped space. Garvan steps back and smiles.

'Don't they look cosy.'

Bray thumps him in the arm and gestures to the third body. 'Even cosier once he joins them.' Bray helps Garvan unceremoniously stuff the man on top of his colleague and Forty-Three. Not quite the Foundation-styled send off the men probably deserved. It's just their bad luck they were in the wrong place at the wrong time. Killing the men didn't sit well with Bray but they had no choice. All doors in and out of the base have palm scan locks fitted.

As soon as Bray and Garvan left Earth as criminals, their identification had been marked. Their palm prints, retinal scans, and any other means of identification was permanently flagged. If they were caught, they'd be back in prison before they knew what was happening—if they were lucky. Escaped convicts infiltrating Earth without permission is bad enough. Add killing Forty-Three and the other men to that, and it probably earned them a place at the top of the most wanted list.

Garvan makes sure the panel is secured back on the wall while Bray packs his own clothes into the bag at his feet. Garvan passes him the guns they borrowed from the men. Bray hides their Outer Sector weapons in the bag under their clothes then pushes the Foundation issued weapon into the holster on his hip. He stands up and takes a deep breath.

'Ready for this?'

Garvan rubs his hands together. 'Can't wait.' He

looks around the small storage room. 'Still wish we had time to cause some mayhem here. Seems a shame to miss such a great opportunity.'

'I hear you. Our best chance of getting off the ship in one piece is as soon as she lands. We need to jump ship along with the rest of the crew. There's less chance of us standing out in a large group.'

Garvan nods but is far from happy. 'I just wanted to have a little fun before we leave, is that so wrong?'

'We'll come back and destroy something later. Will that make you happy?'

'I'll hold you to that.' Garvan grins and nods. 'Fair enough. Lead the way.'

They step out of the relative safety of the storage room and enter the vast cargo hold on *Alpha*. Her enormous loading ramp is lowered, showing an enormous hangar housing the ship. Dozens of drones march up and down the ramp, carrying boxes of supplies in and out of the ship. A gleaming transport is being loaded with some of the heavier crates taken from the new colony. Bray's eyes narrow as he tries to make out the details on the boxes. One of them holds the Scientist's personal computer along with all the data from every procedure he carried out.

Like damaging the ship, the cargo from the new colony will have to wait. It tears at Bray to walk away and leave it here, but again, they have no choice. They're just two men and they need to get as far from here as possible while they figure out what to do. Bray glares at the crates being loaded onto the shuttle. Whatever happens, he will locate and destroy the data from the Scientist's system. There's no way he's leaving Earth if the Foundation have the knowledge and ability to make more cyborgs, to destroy more lives for their own personal gain. The experiments have to stop. No one else should have to suffer like himself and Gryffin have.

Garvan nudges him in the side discretely. 'One foot in front of the other, Commander. You're looking a tad suspicious.'

Bray nods and clutches the strap of the bag in his hand. Full of illegal weapons, Outer Sector clothes, and two severed hands, he can't afford to let it go for even a second. He straightens his shoulders and strides through the cargo hold towards the ramp. It appears luck is on their side. The cargo bay is so busy with transports entering and leaving in quick succession they manage to slip out unnoticed. Using a transport as cover, they keep pace beside it as it exits the ship and travels along the length of the far wall.

Bray tries to focus on where he's going but his eyes continue to wander around the space they are in. In stark contrast to Ultar's crude stone hangar, the Foundation base is made of highly polished, immaculate metal. Powerful lights embedded in the towering ceiling bathe every inch of the space in a harsh white light. Lines and lines of fighters and cargo vessels take up the entire right side of the hangar and occupy the numerous levels like a giant beehive. Human and drone technicians mill around the ships seeing to repairs and maintenance.

'Ultar doesn't stand a chance against this,' Bray mutters to Garvan. 'We have to find a way to warn Gryffin and the others.'

'Agreed. How about I ask someone if I can make a call?'

'I'm being serious,' Bray hisses.

'So am I, Commander. Right now, it's our own lives I'm worried about. Stop thinking with your heart. Our first priority is to get out of here. We're no good to anyone as corpses.'

Bray bites the inside of his cheek to stop any reply. Garvan is right and that irritates him.

'So, Commander, any idea where the exit is?'

Bray nods towards the far end of the hangar and the glowing red emergency light. 'Must be down there.' They slip out from behind the automated transport and crouch behind the cargo containers lining the wall. Ducking and diving behind the crates, they near their target. Bray stops all of a sudden and grabs Garvan's arm. 'Wait.'

'Are you serious?' Garvan hisses.

Bray crouches down to examine a crate. He taps his fingers against the side of the box. 'This came from the new colony.'

'That's nice.'

'I'm serious, Garvan.'

'So am I,' he replies, harshly. 'We've talked about this.'

Bray gets to his feet and leans closer to Garvan. 'The cargo is why we were on *Alpha* in the first place. Everything about the cyborg program is on that computer.'

'Yeah, I know. You agreed we had to leave it for the moment. Look around you. We're seriously outnumbered, Commander. I know the Foundation having that information is a bad thing, but if we're going to have any chance of getting out of here, we have to leave it. It's going to be hard enough getting the two of us out without lugging a flipping big crate along for the ride.'

'But—'

'But nothing. Have you forgotten the small matter of a dead cyborg and two personnel hidden in the wall on the ship? Once they're found, they'll know someone hitched a ride. I want to be long gone before they come looking for us. Move!'

Bray opens his mouth to argue, but changes his mind when he sees a group of technicians moving in their direction. 'You're right. Time to go.'

He picks up the bag and aims for the door again. Every step of the way, Bray fully expects someone to shout for them to stop. It seems the buzz created in the bay by the return of *Alpha* is keeping everyone busy. Bray crouches down in front of the door to rummage through the bag while Garvan keeps watch. Bray takes the two hands out and passes one to Garvan. The large man makes a face as he splays the fingers out. 'This brings back memories.'

Bray glances over his shoulder at him. 'You've handled a severed hand before?'

Garvan smiles. 'Long story, Commander. Perhaps when we have more time.'

Bray raises his eyebrows and turns back to the door. He passes one of the two stolen key cards to Garvan. 'You want to go first?'

They hold their breath as Garvan presses the hand against the scanner at the side of the door, and slips the card into the reader. The light above the door turns green and the metal slides silently into the wall. Garvan steps through and the door secures behind him. Bray repeats the procedure with the other man's hand and joins Garvan on the far side.

Bray stares in wonder around him. Instead of the maintenance tunnels he expected, they're in an enormous glass lobby area. The room must be at least ten stories high and made entirely of seamless glass. Their scuffed boots squeak on the highly polished white floor as they cross the vast space.

Garvan attempts to pull the sleeves of his coat down so the cuffs are in the same vicinity as his wrists. 'I feel like we're leaving a trail of grime after us.'

Bray nods. 'I know what you mean. We don't exactly blend in.' He looks around and grimaces when he sees two security personnel and two drones standing at the door to the outer courtyard.

Garvan turns his back to the guards and Bray follows suit. 'Drones randomly scan faces. Don't think they'll like what they discover with us.'

'We have to get out of the open.' Bray gestures to three doors at the back of the lobby and smiles. The door on the left has 'MAINTENANCE PERSONNEL ONLY' stamped on a red plaque attached to the door. 'Best option for us.'

Garvan follows Bray to the door, and after using their acquired hands again, they disappear into the corridor. Garvan stoops to talk quietly to Bray. 'No way we're going to be able to mosey out the front door. Could be a bit risky using the prints out in the open like that. Nothing screams we're trouble quicker than taking a severed hand out of your bag.'

Bray readjusts his cap to make sure his implant is concealed.

'There are drones everywhere. We need to get out of here and regroup. Somewhere away from so many Foundation security measures.' They continue along the maintenance corridor, checking each of the doors they pass for more guards or drones, but they're alone. They reach the last door and Bray pulls the "borrowed" hand out of his pocket and holds it up to the panel. He looks at Garvan and raises an eyebrow. Garvan rests his hand on his gun and nods. Bray places the palm against the panel. The light flashes and Garvan steps outside.

'All clear.'

Bray joins him, blinking as the bright sunlight hits him. Once the spots clear from his vision, Bray finds himself in a large maintenance yard lined with rubbish compacters and recycling units.

Garvan spins and grabs Bray by the arm. They duck down behind the nearest compacter and slump to the ground. Garvan points to the far wall. Bray risks a quick look and sees what caught Garvan's attention. 'Security units, Commander. No doubt motion detectors and facial recognition. Best keep out of the open.'

Bray closes his eyes and takes off the cap. He runs a hand through his sweat-soaked hair and rests his head back against the wall.

What a bloody disaster. Garvan is only in this mess because of him. He should have gone after Forty-Three alone. If he'd acted immediately, Forty-Three would be dead on the landing deck of the colony and Garvan would be in the Outer Sector. Now they're both stuck here and the Foundation still have access to all the data. He presses the heel of his hand against the implant on his face. As if things aren't bad enough, the metal hurts like crazy. The blow from Forty-Three probably did some damage to the useless component.

'You okay?'

He opens his eyes and grimaces at the look of concern on Garvan's face. 'Yeah. We can't stay here. You know anyone in the area?'

Garvan shakes his head. 'Last I heard, my family relocated to the colony on Mars after my arrest.' He smiles but there's little warmth in it. 'Doubt they'd be too welcoming anyway. In their eyes I'm a criminal.'

He rubs the back of his neck as he looks away from Bray. 'Don't get me wrong—I'd give anything to see them. Hell, I'd give my life to see them, but not like this. I want to clear my name before I go anywhere near them.' He shrugs and looks back at Bray. 'You?'

Bray makes a face. He's got family on Earth and that's part of the problem. His uncle, Morgan, was incredibly close to his younger sister, Maggie, and took it especially hard when she died. It didn't help when Bray took a slightly grey path in life. Morgan's wife Shayla had spent most of her time separating the two of them or stepping in when Bray and his cousin Erin got in trouble for doing something they shouldn't have. The last time he saw Morgan, the man had made it clear Bray was a disappointment, and he never wanted to see him again. 'Yeah, like you, I'm not sure how welcomed I'll be.'

Garvan holds up his hands, mimicking scales. 'Uncomfortable family reunion verses being killed by the Foundation.'

Bray looks down and sighs.

Garvan drops his hands and frowns. 'Seriously? What the blazes did you do?'

'Everything I wasn't supposed to... and more. I guess we don't have much choice though.'

Garvan clasps his hands together. 'Fantastic. Uncomfortable family reunion it is. They near here?'

Bray shakes his head. 'That would be too easy. They live a couple of hours from here. We'll need transport of some kind. Stealing a shuttle is out. The

Foundation will have plenty of time to track us down. We'll be picked up before we leave the city limits.' Bray leans back against the unit and chews his bottom lip. Something on the side of the compacter catches his attention. 'I think I have an idea. You're not going to like it though.'

Bray ignores the stench surrounding him and concentrates on the landmarks going by. The surprisingly spotless transport left the base thirty minutes ago on its way to a large recycling facility about an hour's walk from Morgan's house. His slightly shady past saved them. When he was younger, himself and a few equally shady friends had used the compacter transports to smuggle themselves and any contraband they were carrying in and out of the city walls. The trucks were never checked by the elite inside the city walls. Trash and recycling was too far below their station. They simply trusted that the checks were being carried out by the working class outside the walls. In truth, checks were rarely done. The workers couldn't care less.

He's just hoping the main compacter site is still in the same region of the outer city as Morgan's house. They'd have to jump out before the transport reached the site, but fingers crossed, they'd be able to make the rest of the journey on foot without being seen.

He peers out through a narrow slit in the wall of the compacter. The route to the facility takes them down a large, well-maintained road dividing the centre of the city in half. The perfection everywhere is so obvious, it practically screams out to Bray. Each shop and building is immaculate and decorated in soothing pastel colours. Every garden is well tended, with cleanly painted fences separating it from its neighbours. Well-dressed children play calmly and quietly with their friends. Even the few dogs he sees have been groomed to perfection. No dirt tarnishes the pristine paint on the transports parked outside the houses.

The sterile perfection of the inner city is nearly claustrophobic to him. He can't understand how people can live like this. It's part of the reason he never settled on Earth in the first place. Even from a young age, Bray knew the Foundation and their ridiculous class system was wrong. The older he got, the stronger his anger towards them became. What right did a group of council members and a central computer have to dictate your life?

Each birth was logged in their system, and

depending on the results of the testing they underwent in the first few years of school, careers were assigned. How the hell can someone decide that, at the age of seven, you are suited to be a PA for a fat-cat politician? The idea is so ridiculous. Bray struggled with how few people actually argued against the decision. He'd much prefer the freedom and uniqueness of Ultar any day over the rigid conformity on Earth. The sooner he could leave this planet and back to *Perses* the better. He wants nothing to do with Earth or anyone still living under Foundation control—his own family included.

He frowns as Garvan releases a loud snore and mutters in his sleep. Garvan told him he could sleep anywhere. Given their current surroundings, that was an understatement. If he were here by himself, he would have stayed on the base. He would have done whatever he could to take a transport and get back home. He couldn't take that risk with Garvan. The man just got his life back. He doesn't deserve to die because of a stupid mistake Bray made.

As he watches well placed trees and nondescript locals pass by the transport, his mind wanders back to the assault on the colony. He hopes everyone made it out in one piece. Even Gryffin. He spent enough time studying the Nomad leader to know his implants were not in the best shape. A new leg is the least of his problems. Unless they can figure out exactly what the Scientist did to him, they won't be able to stop the malfunctions from killing Gryffin. He may not like his brother, but that doesn't mean he wants him to die.

There's no escaping the truth—somehow, he needs to get that unit back. The Foundation shouldn't have access to the information. If he can find it, Milla can repair Gryffin and then destroy the data. Everything could be put right with that unit.

Bray nudges Garvan. 'You awake?'

'I am now.' Garvan rubs his eyes, grimacing as he picks a piece of wet tissue from his hand. 'Nice. We there yet?'

'Not yet. Didn't really want to get caught because someone overheard your snoring.'

'Yeah because it sounds like an opera when you're snoring.'

Bray waves his hand, signalling for Garvan to stop talking. Bray holds his breath as the transport approaches the main city gates. After less than two minutes, and no checks, they are cleared and leave the city behind. Bray smiles as he gets his first glimpse of a field. It has an enormous house in the centre of it, but it's still greenery. The business men and women, not quite at the level of an elite, live in monstrous houses surrounding the walls. Bray sneers at the properties. They could easily fit a few dozen families in their mansions but he suspects they're still not happy with that much clean, well equipped personal space. The main goal on Earth is to reach the level of an elite and live in the inner city. Nothing else matters to them. It makes him sick.

Bray shakes his head. 'I'm sorry.'

Garvan blinks a few times them props himself up on his elbow. 'You should be. It stinks in here.'

'No, not for this. Okay well, not just for this. I didn't mean to drag you in to this mess.'

Garvan smiles and picks something sticky from his dirty blond hair. 'It's a mess all right.' He shakes his hand, trying to separate himself from whatever it is.

'I didn't—'

'I know. You mean being stranded on Earth and having to stay with your family. They're not that bad, are they?'

'It's not that back and white. I left on bad terms and haven't spoken to them since. I just don't know what sort of reception I'm going to get.'

Garvan smirks. 'Don't worry, Commander. I'll keep you safe.'

'Now I feel so much better, cheers.' He looks back out through the slats and grimaces. 'It's all different, Garvan.'

'What is?'

'Out there. I know it's been a few... well quite a few years since I've been here, but everything has been built on. I'm sure this used to be fields for miles instead of these monstrosities.'

Garvan grimaces. 'Price of progress, my friend. More cities, more prestigious houses, and less fields. I'm sure quite a bit has changed since you left. Did you grow up in the country?'

Bray shakes his head. 'On and off. I relocated out here full time when my parents died.'

'Tell me to mind my own business, but fancy filling me in on what happened?'

Bray shifts in the rubbish, trying to get more comfortable. He finally gives up and looks back at Garvan, hoping he's moved on from the conversation.

'Well?' Garvan asks.

'Well what?'

'I need to know what I'm heading in to, Commander.'

'It's nothing to worry about, just family stuff.'

Garvan laughs. 'You trying to convince me or yourself? You didn't look this on edge heading into battle with the Foundation. Is it really that bad?'

'I wasn't exactly the model son. To them, I'm a criminal, always have been. The last time I saw Morgan was from the back of a security transport on my way to a new life far away from them.' Bray snorts and shakes his head. 'Not the best memory.'

Garvan frowns. 'Sorry, Commander. That's a bit rough. What did you do?'

Bray leans back against the side wall, not caring about what he's lying against. 'Why do you want to know?'

Garvan stretches his legs out in front of him and crosses his arms. 'Got time to kill.'

'Yeah, well you'll have to kill it another way. It's none of your damn business.'

Garvan holds up his hands. 'Fair enough, Commander.' He turns away from Bray and closes his eyes. 'This time wait until we're there before you wake me up.'

∞

Bray ducks as Garvan sails through the air, landing in a heap in front of him. 'You okay?'

Garvan smirks as he dusts off his clothes. 'Fine and dandy, sir. Never jumped from a moving recycling transport before. You sure know how to show me the sights in style.'

Bray laughs. 'Only the best for you.' Bray warily stands up and checks their surroundings. Now this is more like it. The farming sector is the only place on Earth he can tolerate. He frowns as he looks around him. 'Nice.'

Garvan stands beside him, his hands on his hips. 'What?'

'This used to be farms and fields. Some of the landscape rings some bells, but for the most part, a lot has altered. This should be acres of fields with a scattering of houses. Not this.'

In front of them is a new development. The large site has taken over the farmland, marring the wide open space with sterile houses. The site is still under development but there must be a few dozen properties. Garvan takes a few steps closer to the new houses and whistles. 'Beautiful eyesore.'

Bray grunts. 'As you said—price of progress.' He slowly trudges along the deserted street cutting through the houses. 'Give me empty fields any day.'

'They're big places. Must be for important people.'

'A piece of country living for the rich, city fat-cats.'

'Correct me if I'm wrong but don't you need a little bit of grass to qualify for the country?' He stops and examines one of the houses. 'The design is good, just boring as hell.' Garvan shrugs. 'Actually, it's probably a perfect fit!'

Bray doesn't respond. Although he spent years clashing with Morgan and his insistence on Bray working the land with him, he's heartbroken at what he sees. The Foundation was so intent on dominating everything they could, they we're abusing and neglecting what they have. The last thing Earth needed was more buildings.

Garvan grabs him by the arm pulling him face down in the dirt behind a storage shed. Bray spits out a mouthful of dust and is about to complain when he hears it—the sound of a small engine nearing their location. Garvan puts a finger to his lips and points to the door of the shed. Bray quietly pulls at the makeshift door, muttering a silent thank you as it opens for him. They crawl inside and hold their breaths as the sound gets closer. Bray peers out of a missing knot in the wooden door and finally sees it.

From what he can make out, it's a camera on a small airborne drone. The camera slowly examines the area they were standing in a minute ago before moving along the side of the house. Bray pulls back from the door as it comes to a stop in front of the hole, the red beam from the camera piercing the darkness. Pressed tightly to either side of the shed, they are out of its range, but Bray remains rigid just in case. His heart thumps loudly in his chest as the red beam shifts from side to side. With his eyes, he gestures towards the bag of guns on the ground at his feet. Garvan slowly shifts his head from one side to the other in a silent no.

Eventually, the drone pulls back, its engines growing fainter as it travels down the road. Bray finally releases the breath he was holding. He rolls his shoulders trying to ease the stiffness. 'What the hell was that?' he asks, his voice hushed.

Garvan licks his dry lips. 'Scout drone. They must have come into service after you left. The larger humanoid drones patrol the city and those pesky guys take the outer areas. They're in constant contact with the HQ.'

'That why you didn't want me to shoot it?'

'Wouldn't have done a thing except alert them that we're here. C'mon, we should bury the hands here then get moving.'

For a building site, there's no equipment lying around, so Bray and Garvan dig a deep hole with some scrap metal. 'You think we should dump the uniforms too?' Garvan asks.

Bray shakes his head in disagreement. 'Leather is reserved for the elite. We go wandering around the countryside wearing leather trousers, we'll just bring more attention to ourselves. We should be safe enough when we reach Morgan's.'

Garvan stretches his arms above his head and smiles as the underside of each arm rips in protest. 'Don't give me that look. If I'm stuck in this for a bit longer I need more room. Damn thing is cutting off my blood supply.'

They deposit the hands and bury them, hiding the newly dug soil with some empty crates Garvan found down the side of one of the houses.

They continue along the road, keeping tight to the houses. Garvan glances over at Bray and chuckles. 'Got a bit of dirt on your face.'

Bray wipes his face. 'Where?'

Garvan points to his cheek, then his forehead, then his nose. 'Hell, it's everywhere.'

Bray uses the bottom of the jacket to wipe his face, grimacing as he remembers too late that his coat is smothered in the aromas from the compacter. 'Damn it.'

'Hey, it could work in our favour. The drone might think you're a pile of trash.'

'You could have just nudged me to the side.'

Garvan nods. 'That I could have, but I didn't want to risk your life. Thought it would be best to—'

'Shove my face in the dirt?'

Garvan shrugs. 'A man's got to have some fun, Commander. So, you haven't spoken to your family since you were taken away?'

'Subtle change of subject.' Bray shakes his head. 'They tried to contact me on Vana, but I wasn't interested.'

'Ah, so you were sulking like a real man.'

Bray glares over his shoulder at Garvan. 'I was seventeen. I thought I was in the right. Anyway, by the time I figured out I was being an idiot, too much time had passed.' He shrugs and kicks a stone out of his path. 'I guess it was easier to move on.'

'But you didn't, right.'

Bray stops and turns to face Garvan. 'What is this? Amateur psychology with Garvan.'

He shrugs. 'Seems to me you've got some issues, Commander.'

'Yeah and I'm looking at one of them right now.'

'Family issues I mean. Have you thought about Gryffin?'

Bray shakes his head and turns away. He focuses on the horizon and begins walking again.

'Ignoring it won't make it go away.'

'I'm not ignoring it, I'm ignoring you, hoping you'll go away.'

Garvan smirks. 'Sorry, you're stuck with me. Stop avoiding the question.'

Bray waves his arms in the air and spins around again. 'Would you just let it drop. There's enough shit going on without bringing dead brothers in to it. There's a very strong chance Uncle Morgan could call the Foundation as soon as he sees me. Even if he lets us in the door, I'm still not off the hook. He's going to want to know where I've been and what I've been doing.'

'And?'

'He's a farmer and a law abiding citizen. There's no way he can accept that I spent years lying, stealing and cheating my way around the Sector before being broken out of prison to lie and cheat my way onto a Hunter ship where I lied to my captain for years so I could help the Foundation conceal a bigger lie that involved my dead brother.'

Garvan places his hands on his hips and makes a face. 'You may have a point. Doesn't sound the best when you put it like that.'

'Listen, I just want to get us out of the open and in relative safety while I figure out what the hell to do. Gryffin and all that other stuff isn't even entering my mind. Got it?'

Garvan nods and heads down the road. Bray falls into step beside him. He may have sounded convincing but it's far from how he feels. Being back on Earth is bringing up enough memories as it is. The thought of seeing Morgan, Shayla, and Erin again terrifies him. He left that life behind him twelve years ago. As soon as he left Earth, the person he used to be died. How could he go back to that world after everything he's done? He's not ashamed of who he is, but that doesn't mean he wants anything to do with the life he lost. Going back is only going to remind him of everything he could have had if he hadn't left his family.

Bray comes to a stop outside one of the houses. 'Fancy bunking down in here?'

Garvan frowns as he looks around them. 'This is a

building site.'

'What's wrong? Don't like slumming it?'

Garvan runs a hand through his grime-streaked hair. 'Well you know how dust plays havoc with my hair.' Garvan thumps Bray in the arm. 'It's a building site which means there'll be workers back to finish. There's also a strong chance the drone will come back. HQ will know no one should be on site. It's too much of a risk.' He jabs a finger in Bray's chest. 'Quit stalling, Commander. Grow a damn backbone and walk. Your relatives await.'

Bray resists the powerful urge to argue, but the look on Garvan's face tells him it would be a wasted effort. His companion has the irritating ability of being able to see right through him. 'Sometimes I wish I'd left you where I found you.'

Garvan smiles and points down the road. 'Me too. The cockroaches were a lot less argumentative.'.

3

Bray peers around the tree. Garvan leans over and peeks out over Bray's head. 'Couldn't you have found your own tree to hide behind?'

Garvan laughs. 'You got the best one. How does it look?'

Bray nods. 'Quiet.' His uncle's house hadn't changed since he last saw it. Apart from the hulking development down the road, it's as if time has stood still. The neatly painted, old fashioned farmhouse rests at the end of a long winding track lined with trees. An open courtyard circles the front of the property with a white gate leading up the front path to the porch. He looks up at the window to the far left over the porch and smiles. The tile under the sill is still cracked from when he accidentally kicked it while sneaking out one night.

'So, we going to play hide-and-seek all day or are you going to be a big boy and knock on the door?'

'You know, I can always leave you here when I clear out.'

Garvan grins widely then shoves Bray towards the house. 'Coast is clear.'

Bray bites back his reply and continues his approach. Even though the front of the house is sheltered from the road, he still keeps an eye out. He unbolts the gate, wincing as it creaks. Garvan carefully fastens it after them as Bray slowly climbs the steps to the porch. He laughs out loud when he sees a stone dog sitting beside the front door. He and Erin had found the statue at a recycling yard and had insisted on keeping it. Morgan and Shayla hated the damn thing but allowed them to keep it. Bray pats the stone head. 'Good to see you, boy.'

He catches Garvan shaking his head, but ignores him. He faces the door and, before he can chicken out, presses the panel. He hears the chime sound inside the house and he immediately tenses as heavy footsteps approach the door.

The door whips back and Uncle Morgan's mouth drops open. His thick black hair is styled the same way it was years ago and is flecked with grey. His piercing blue eyes are still as vibrant as he examines every inch of Bray. He rubs his greying stubble as he examines Bray from head to toe. Bray opens his mouth to address the man in front of him, but the door is slammed in his face.

Garvan clutches his hand to his heart and sighs. 'That was beautiful, Bray. Really touching.'

Bray glares at Garvan then takes a deep breath before he knocks again.

Morgan swings the door back. He steps closer and examines Bray like he's an irritating stray dog that refuses to get the hint. He pokes Bray in the chest, forcing the young man back a step. 'Thought you might have been a figment of my overactive imagination.'

'I'm real, Morgan.'

The man grunts. 'That's what I'm afraid of.'

'Can we come in?'

Morgan takes a deep breath, but doesn't reply.

'Please, Morgan. I know you're upset with me—'

Morgan snorts and tilts his head to frown up at Bray. 'Upset! You think I'm upset? Twelve years, Brayden. Twelve long years without even so much as one word of communication from you. We went to your memorial service.'

Bray's mouth drops. 'I'm dead?'

'Of course you're dead. Or were dead. The last we heard you were seen at Tyrat prison. You were reported dead after a prison brawl. That's why we had a memorial service for you.' He points down the road. 'Got you a nice spot with the rest of your family. Such a tragedy—mother, father, and two sons dead and not one body recovered. There's a plaque on the wall for the four of you. That's all we have—a lousy plaque.'

'Well, I'm not dead. Can I come in?' Morgan braces his arm against the door-frame, blocking the way. Bray looks over his shoulder as a transport takes off further down the road. 'I'll explain everything, but can you please let us in?'

Morgan nods towards Garvan. 'Who's your friend?'

'For heaven's sake, will you just let us in?'

The older man slaps Bray across the side of his head. 'You can lose that attitude for one. You may be bigger than me but I can still try to kick some sense in to you.'

Bray rubs the side of his head, ignoring the snicker of laughter from Garvan. 'I'm sorry, okay. This is Garvan, he's a friend.'

The man grasps Garvan's hand. 'I'm Morgan. I have the extreme pleasure of being Bray's Uncle. Get in before the neighbours notice you two.'

Bray steps in to the house and is instantly drawn back in to his past. Morgan notices his expression. 'What?'

'Nothing's changed.'

Morgan casts a critical eye over him. 'Seems to me a lot has changed.' He wrinkles his nose and takes a step back.' What the hell is that smell?'

Bray sniffs himself. 'Sorry. We had to hitch a ride to get here unnoticed.'

'Unnoticed in Foundation uniforms? Sounds like a

great plan.' He points to the doorway at the right side of the corridor. 'Go in there but do not touch a damn thing. I don't want the place stinking to high heaven. I'll lock the doors so no one strolls in on you two in my house.'

Morgan disappears through the door at the end of the hallway. Garvan raises an eyebrow as he looks at Bray. 'Touching reunion.'

'C'mon.' Bray leads him into the large, and bright living room. Comfortable, worn leather chairs line the wall facing the enormous fireplace. Bray remembers being able to stand up in the recess when he was younger. Bray and his older cousin, Erin, would spend hours scaling the chimney, each one trying to outdo the other. Garvan looks at the line of photos along the mantle. He chuckles and points to the frame on the far left.

'Please tell me that's you.'

Bray examines the picture. The small, dark-haired child smiling at the camera is him—although a much more innocent version. 'Any more sounds like that from you and I'll take serious offence.'

Garvan nods, but clearly has no intention of behaving. Bray picks up another frame from beside his. It must have been taken just before Daegan left for the school trip. He may have tried to ignore the resemblance to the brother he vaguely remembers, but seeing the photo brings it all home to him. If you put the picture beside Gryffin, no one could deny they're the same person, no matter how much you want to.

Bray turns away from the photos and lowers into the nearest chair just as Morgan returns and stands in the doorway with his arms crossed. 'Out of the chair! So, what do you want?'

Bray gets to his feet, suddenly feeling uncomfortable. 'We've got nowhere else to go.'

'So you decide to darken my doorway? Nice welcome home present, Brayden.'

'Please, Morgan. We need your help. I'm only asking for a few days to figure out what we're going to do.'

Morgan relaxes slightly and leans against the door-frame. He stares in silence at the two men. Bray notices that even the unmovable Garvan is feeling the power of Morgan's stern glare. 'If it looks like you're attracting attention, you both go. Immediately.'

Bray nods quickly. 'Of course. Thanks.'

Morgan grunts as he turns around and plods up the worn wooden stairs. He stops on the third step and looks over his shoulder. 'Get away from my furniture until you've both been disinfected. You going to follow me or what?'

They both leap to attention, hurrying up the stairs and along the top floor of the old farmhouse. Morgan stops at the first door and ushers Garvan inside. 'You can use this room. There's an en-suite and the bed is freshly made.' Morgan looks critically at his ill-fitting Foundation uniform. 'I'm guessing you're not going through a sudden growth spurt.' Garvan opens his mouth to reply but Morgan holds up a hand. 'Forget I asked. I'll try to find you something else.'

'I've got our clothes in here,' Bray says, holding up the bag he took from *Alpha*.

'If they smell as bad as you, you'll not be wearing them in my house. Hand them over, I'll put them through the cleaner while you're getting ready.'

Bray crouches down and pulls their clothes out, keeping the weapons out of sight in the bottom of the bag. He holds the bundle of rancid clothes out to Morgan, who grips them at arm's length from his body. 'I'll have these back to you in half an hour.' He stops at the door and gestures down the corridor. 'You can use your old room.'

'Thanks, Morgan. Hey, where's Shayla?'

Morgan pauses at the top step, his gaze focused on the bottom of the stairs. One look at Morgan's face tells him everything he needs to know. A cold dread settles in his stomach. He slumps back against the wall, his legs suddenly unable to support him. 'No...'

Morgan glances at him quickly, unshed tears glistening in his hard eyes. 'Two years ago last month.'

'What... what happened?'

Morgan straightens his shoulders and turns his harsh gaze back to Bray. 'What does it matter to you? You left Earth without giving her or the rest of your family a second thought. Get cleaned up. Dinner is in an hour.'

Without another word, Morgan disappears

downstairs. Garvan places his hand on Bray's shoulder but he doesn't want the comfort. Bray pulls out of his grasp and wanders down the corridor towards his old room. He shoves the door aside, shuts it behind him and slides to the floor, hugging his knees to his chest as he cries.

4

Bray steps out of the shower feeling a little more human. He used the time to let out his anguish over Shayla. He can't accept the fact she's gone. No matter how bad things got when he was younger, she was always there for him. After his parents' death, Morgan was the strength, the disciplinarian, while Shayla was the comfort. He's not embarrassed to admit there was many a day when a simple hug from his aunt could make the dark clouds disappear. He can't get his head around this house without the smell of her cooking, without her smile when you walked in the door or eating meals without her refereeing the bickering between the cousins. He slams his hand against the sink. This house, this family has lost its heart.

He meets his reflection in the mirror. He should have been here for her, for Morgan, and for Erin. Instead he was in the middle of Avoca's cyborg mess, chasing after an experiment that suddenly turned into his long lost brother. He looks down at the sink. He hopes Shayla didn't die thinking he couldn't give a damn about her. The worst thing is, he can't even apologise to her. He delayed coming back for too long. He looks back at his reflection. It's too late to do anything about it now. The only thing he can do for his family is get the hell away from here before the Foundation came looking for them.

He takes a deep breath then splashes cold water on his face to deal with his reddened eyes. Unfortunately, now that he's clean, the colourful pattern of bruises stands out harshly against his skin. Forty-Three gave him one hell of a beating before Garvan took him out. He presses a hand to his ribs, hissing in pain as the muscles protest. Nothing's broken, but the bruising will stay with him for a while.

He stares at his reflection in the mirror over the sink. He looks terrible. He came back from the dead looking like he actually came back from the dead. No wonder Morgan wasn't too keen to let them in. He rolls his stiff shoulders and grimaces as one of the wounds on his chest protests by opening up again. He dabs the blood with a cloth, pressing it to his skin until the bleeding eases. Satisfied he's not going to drip blood across the floor, he throws the cloth with his pile of clothes and rummages through the cupboards under the sink for a first aid kit. He'd been in so many scuffles growing up that Shayla left a fully stocked kit in his room at all times.

He yelps as a sharp pain stabs through his eye and extends out to the implant. He places a hand against the sink to stop himself plunging forwards. Bray gasps and presses his hand to his face. After a few seconds it eases and he slowly pulls himself to his feet. He takes a couple of deep breaths then leans forward to examine his eye in the mirror. His right eye is as it should be, but his left eye looks strange. It takes him a few seconds to realise that, instead of having a brown iris, his has a tinge of blue mixed in. He manoeuvres closer to the mirror and opens his eye as wide as he can, wincing as his implant throbs.

'What the hell?'

Whatever just happened, he knows it can't be good. He spent weeks in a coma after his time with the Scientist and, during that time, had undergone rigorous testing. He got the all clear. Milla assured him that, as far as she could tell, his implants weren't active. He's not doubting her, but after seeing everything the Scientist was capable of, he can't help wonder if he did something Milla couldn't detect. The metal has always hurt, but he knows he just has to learn to live with it, like Gryffin does. Recently, the pain had evolved. Instead of a dull ache, it sometimes felt like a thick spike was being shoved into his eye.

He drops his head and shoves back against the sink. There's enough going on in his life without adding this to the mess. He makes a second attempt at hunting for the med kit, locates what he's looking for, wraps a towel around his waist and carries the kit back to his bed. He empties the kit on the bed and frowns at the contents. Instead of bandages, tape and suture packs, there's a tube of ointment and a metal case with a scanner of some kind in it. He must be out of touch with Foundation technology. Just as he's about to throw it back under the sink, a knock on the door interrupts him.

'Yeah?'

'I've got clean clothes.'

'Come in,' Bray replies before he can stop himself. Morgan steps into the room and freezes when he gets a good look at him.

'Oh my God,' he exclaims. Morgan stares at Bray, making him feel like he's under a microscope. He should have kept covered up while he was here. His uncle's face shows a mix of surprise, shock, and disgust as he examines him. Fresh from the shower, his wet hair is brushed back off his face showing the implant against his eye. The large metal plate screwed to his chest over his heart is on full display along with a nice peppering of bruises and cuts from the fight. If all that wasn't bad enough, his newly acquired Hunter tattoo's wrapped around both arms, his chest and his back, add their swirling black lines to everything else Morgan has to take in.

'What the hell have you done to yourself, boy?'

Bray rolls his eyes at Morgan's name for him. Even after all these years it still rubs him the wrong way. He looks for something to hide his chest with but his clean clothes are still clutched in his uncle's arms. 'Can I please have my clothes?'

Morgan steps into the room, his gaze narrowed as he looks at Bray. 'What happened to you, Brayden? Do you not think you've done enough without mutilating yourself too?'

Bray stands up and faces his uncle. He hates the small kick of satisfaction he gets from the fear that momentarily shows on Morgan's face. 'Typical. You've already judged the situation without hearing even one small fact. You that eager to put me down?'

'The facts are screwed to your flesh and permanently marking your skin. Why Bray? What happened to make you do this to yourself?'

'You think I wanted metal screwed into my flesh? I was strapped down to a table and experimented on like a damn lab rat!'

The deathly silence that follows his unplanned outburst fills the room like an unseen presence. He risks a quick look at Morgan and cringes at the horror plastered over his face. Morgan takes a step closer. 'Experimented on?'

'Forget it.'

'I can't just forget it. What the hell happened?' Morgan asks.

'I said forget it!'

Morgan's expression blanks as he silently stares at Bray. 'Very well, Brayden. Have it your way.' Then, with a curt nod, he dumps the pile of clean clothes on the chair by the door.

Bray slumps back on the bed and curses loudly. It's only after he lowers his hands from his face that he notices Morgan is sitting beside him on the bed. 'I don't want to keep fighting, okay.'

'Finally, something we can agree on.' Morgan's eyes travel over Bray's body before settling on the large cut on his chest. 'Do you want me to see to that? I don't want you to bleed all over your clean clothes.'

Bray nods briskly then points to the kit on the bed. 'I'm a little out of date.'

Morgan holds up the device and frowns. 'This? This is years out of date. I've been meaning to get a new one, but with things the way they are, I keep forgetting.'

'What things?'

Morgan shakes his head apologetically. 'Another time. For now, let's patch you up. Should I ask about the other guy?'

'Probably best you don't. I'd like to keep you on my side. I don't have a lot of friends left on Earth.'

'Dead men don't generally have friends—just people who vaguely remember them.' Morgan squeezes some clear ointment from the tube onto his finger. 'This may sting a little, although, by the look of your chest you can handle a lot more than a sting.'

Bray smiles but doesn't reply. Now's not the time to open up, if ever.

Morgan gently smothers the wound with the gel then turns on the device. A beam of red light shoots out of one end. Morgan directs the light over Bray's wound and slowly works it along the wound. 'It's deep. It'll probably take a few minutes to heal. So, I couldn't help but notice, you and your mate have leather trousers and jackets. You two royalty or something?'

Bray laughs. 'Believe me, far from it. I've been in the Outer Sector. We still farm animals out there.'

Morgan openly stares at Bray. 'For food and clothes?'

'Sure. It's how the locals make a living.'

Morgan raises his eyebrows. 'I have to admit, I'm a little jealous. Appeals to the trapped farmer in me.'

'Yeah, it has its moments.' Bray winces as the device stings. 'So, where's Erin?'

Morgan frowns as he concentrates on his task. 'She's at work.'

'She still lives here?'

Morgan shakes his head. 'Erin has an apartment in the city, but spends most of her down time here on the farm if she can. If I'm being honest, she's spending less time here than she used to.'

'Has she made you a proud grandfather yet?'

Morgan laughs and Bray can't help smile. He didn't realise how much he missed his uncle's rare light-hearted laugh. 'Erin? No. She's all work and no play, I'm afraid. She's doing well, but…' he glances up at Bray. 'I guess I miss the carefree little girl she used to be.'

'Don't think carefree is a word you ever used when we got in to trouble. And from what I remember, she got in almost as much trouble as me.'

'Almost,' he agrees. 'She changed after Daegan died. You were young so you probably don't remember, but it hit her hard. Then things happened with you… You and Daegan were like brothers to her. She lost one and then the other. When Shayla… well, I'm not surprised it got to her.'

Bray finds it hard to believe Erin is so different. She was like a surrogate sister to him growing up. Both cousins would lead each other astray at every opportunity. Having one or both of them outside the headmaster's office was a daily occurrence. Bray knows that's why he was eventually sent away. Morgan was afraid his beloved daughter was being led astray by her younger cousin. When it came down to it, he made the right decision in picking her over Bray.

'I'm sorry, Morgan.'

He looks up at him. 'For what exactly?'

'I shouldn't have come here.'

Morgan shrugs. 'Yeah well, you're here now. No point going on about it.'

'If the Foundation catch on that—'

Morgan nods and blows out a breath. 'You were right before. It's best I don't know what happened or what you're running from.' He wipes an antiseptic cloth over the wound. Bray glances down, amazed to see a pink scar where the cut was only a few minutes ago.

Morgan packs the device away and gets to his feet. 'You can use the unit in my office. Erin has a privacy lock on it so the Foundation shouldn't be able to see what you're doing. I don't know if it'll even get off the ground, but your old transport is still in the barn too. Might be worth a look. Anything you need just let me know. It's best you figure out how to get back to your people as soon as possible.'

Morgan shuts the door behind him leaving Bray alone in his old room, feeling like an unwelcome stranger in his own life.

One places his cocktail on the small glass table beside his chair. He looks over at his two grandchildren playing in his large swimming pool. His step-daughter and her family arrived earlier that day and he's enjoying some well-deserved family time after setting up the new colony. The sound of his new wife and step-daughter laughing carries from the kitchen as they prepare lunch. He closes his eyes and leans back in his chair turning his face towards the warm sun.

While he enjoys being with his family, his main concern at the moment is the project. The team of personnel tasked with carrying out every wish and command of the Council are competent enough, but the project is too important for him to trust to other people. Especially Leeson. He's not sure any of them have the stomach to follow the project through to the end. There will be some unpleasant decisions to be made in the coming weeks. Decisions that would be imperative to their success. He's not too worried though. Leeson will do what is needed or he will be removed from the group. Something Leeson will do whatever he can to avoid. Once removed from the Foundation he would be forced to live on one of the colony worlds in the Outer Sector. He'd have to leave behind his large house, comfortable life and wealth to live in a farming village growing his own food and undertaking labour to survive—possibly having to look to groups like the Nomad for protection.

He smiles to himself, lying back in his lounger with his hands clasped behind his head. The Nomad will be obsolete soon enough. Once the Foundation complete the new colony they will have a visible presence in the Sector. Any rebels will have to conform or relocate. By the end of the year the Foundation will have at least another fifteen worlds under their protection. The rest of the Sector will fall into their grasp within a few months of that. The Nomad will all be dead or in prison, well apart from their esteemed leader of course. No matter what it takes or what he has to do, he will have the prototype back under his complete control again. Once that happens, anyone who chooses to defy the Foundation and take sides with the rebels will be dealt with by the young man. One scratches his stomach as he laughs out loud. Roman and the rest of the crew from Infinity will soon regret their decision once a very angry cyborg is sent after them.

His laughter dies away when his personal unit sounds from the polished table beside his head. He ignores it hoping whoever it is will leave him alone, but the irritating sound still buzzes in his ear, interrupting his peace. He opens one eye and locates the unit before closing his eye again. He hits the panel on the side to keep the video off and answers the call. 'This had better be a life and death situation.'

His irritation grows as he hears Leeson fumble with his words. 'Of course. I mean, yes sir, it is.'

Something in Leeson's tone sends alarm bells ringing in his head. He sits up, wraps a towel around his waist then hurries to his home office. He opens the large patio door and steps into the air conditioned room, closing the door behind him to shut out the sounds of laughter from the pool. 'What is it?'

'Sir, the recon vessel just arrived back from the new colony.'

'And? For God's sake man, stop delaying and just report!'

'And it's been lost, sir.'

One collapses back into the nearest chair and wipes a hand across his clammy brow. 'How is that possible? We had a full armada there to protect the site. When *Alpha* left we had the upper hand. How can a band of rebels in clapped out old ships take the colony?'

Leeson trips over his words again. 'I don't know, sir. Only one of the automated drones made it back. Sir, there was a message recorded on the drone. It said, "Keep out of our sector".

One resists the urge to shout and throw the unit into the glass doors. Not wanting to upset his grandchildren, he takes a few deep breaths while he gets himself together. 'We still have the full shipment from *Alpha*?'

'Yes, sir. But...'

'What else can there possibly be?'

'Sir, it appears two members of her crew are... well, missing, sir.'

'So they decided to disembark mid trip?'

'No, sir. From what the techs can determine so far, their hands left.'

One opens his eyes and stares down at the blank screen. 'You are making even less sense than usual. I suggest you tell me exactly what happened before I decide you are not worth bothering with.'

'Of course. Sir, their palm prints operated a door leaving the cargo hold and accessing the maintenance yard, but they never reported to their superiors. In fact, no one has seen them since they entered *Alpha* on the new colony. Apart from their palm prints, they have disappeared.'

One gets up and looks out of the window at his family. 'Find out what happened. Check every camera on and off the base. Fill out a report and make sure the Council have it available within the hour.'

He shuts down the comms and, unable to resist the urge, hurls his unit at the antique, glass-door display cabinet behind his desk.

∞

Bray steps down from the wide veranda and scuffs his boots in the dry soil. He closes his eyes and lets the smells and sounds of his childhood soothe him. Every conversation with Morgan ended the same way—some things just never change.

'Glad to see you're still alive.'

Bray laughs as Garvan's deep rumble disturbs his peace. 'I was enjoying the moment.'

'Careful, Commander, you wouldn't want me to think you have a softer side.'

Bray glances at his companion. 'You really want to push me?'

Garvan raises his hands and takes a step away. 'Forget I said anything. I probably shouldn't kick a man when he's well and truly down.'

He knows Garvan is just trying to lighten the awkward situation so he doesn't react. 'You smell better.'

'Right back at you. Listen, I'm sorry about your aunt.'

Bray smiles and nods. 'Yeah, me too.'

'You've got a real nice family there, Bray.'

Bray looks out over the horizon. The large cityscape sprawls as far as the eye can see in either direction. 'Yeah, that's why I'm not keen on staying here longer than we have to. We both have first-hand experience of being on the wrong side of the Foundation.'

'I agree. Problem is, I'm having trouble coming up with a way off this planet.'

'I know. We have no Foundation ID's, no credits, no transport and no way to get home or to safely stay here.'

'Is that all? I thought we were in trouble.'

'You're seriously not all there, you know that?'

Garvan grins. 'Laugh or cry, Commander. Laugh or cry.' In spite of his comment, Garvan's face drops slightly. 'After everything I've been through, everything that's happened, I never thought I'd end up back here again.'

Bray looks over at his companion. 'I'll figure something out. I promise, whatever happens, I will get you back to the Outer Sector.'

Garvan smiles. 'Hey, that wasn't a dig. Just thinking about how things have turned out. I'm not expecting you to know how to get off the surface.'

Bray rests his arms on the wooden railing and rubs his hands together. 'There has to be a way. The Foundation can't have the entire planet locked down.'

Garvan snorts. 'Wouldn't be too sure about that, mate. I wouldn't put anything past them. What about *Perses*? You think Sayber would take the plunge?'

Bray makes a face as he collects his thoughts. He did wonder that himself. It's not like Sayber isn't crazy enough to do it. 'I'm not going to hazard a guess to what goes on in his head. For now, we have to assume it's just us two.'

'Fair enough. Hey, I know it's far from being my business, but have you had any thoughts about the whole Gryffin still being alive situation? You should tell them the truth.'

Bray looks back at the horizon. 'It's not exactly the easiest of subjects to bring up.'

'Morgan took your rise from the dead pretty well, considering.'

'What happened to Gryffin is different. Too bloody different. Morgan looked at my two implants as if they're something sinister, something to be feared and he doesn't even know what they are. Gryffin is in a whole other league. And even if I tell him, it's not like he can meet him. Gryffin can't come here and Morgan will die before he leaves this farm.'

'That may be true, but it changes nothing. You have to tell him.'

Bray spins to face Garvan. 'Don't you think I know that? For now, we say nothing. There's no point reminiscing about Gryffin if we're going to rot here with his memory. Besides, unless we destroy the Scientist's files, cyborgs may become part of day-to-day life. I'm not ready for that to happen. Are you?'

'You know I'm with you, Bray. I've got your back. It just seems to me there are a lot of ghosts wandering around this place, ghosts that could veer you off course. Might be easier for everyone if they were all released so they can be dealt with.'

Bray grabs Garvan by the front of his shirt and his hazel eyes drill into him. 'Keep your nose out of my family's business. You got that?'

Garvan nods once. 'Yes, Commander. I got it, but I'm not agreeing with your reasoning.'

'Disobeying orders now?'

Garvan jabs a thick finger in Bray's chest. 'You've got my loyalty, Commander, but that doesn't mean I'm going to be a damn puppet. If you're looking for someone to follow your orders without question, you've got the wrong person. I'm not an idiot, Commander. I suggest you don't treat me like one.'

Bray slowly takes a step back. 'See what information you can get on the transport hubs around the city. No searches that would raise alarms. Well, unless you think that task is above you.'

Garvan salutes sharply and turns away before Bray can comment.

Bray peers around the edge of his bedroom window as the sleek black transport comes to a stop outside the farmhouse. His stomach clenches as he stares at the stationary vehicle. He's not looking forward to meeting the driver.

The door lifts and a tall, dark-haired woman steps out. His cousin, Erin, is a lot different than he remembers. Then again, they all are. Erin's eyes take in everything around her as she locks the vehicle and unbolts the heavy wooden gate. Something about her posture, her behaviour triggers alarms in Bray's head. He stupidly never asked what Erin's role is, but after only seeing her for a few seconds, Bray has a horrible feeling he knows what it is and it has nothing to do with sitting behind a desk in an office.

He pulls the bag out from under his bed, loads one of the guns and tucks it in his waistband before creeping along the corridor to Garvan's room. Without knocking, he cracks the door open and slips inside. Garvan is at his window, frowning at the vehicle. 'That Erin?'

Bray nods. 'Something ringing alarms bells with you too?'

'She's military,' Garvan replies, confirming Bray's fears. He lifts up his shirt, showing he's taken the same precautions as Bray. He pats the handle of the gun. 'I'm not planning on shooting your cousin, but better safe than sorry.'

Both men freeze as the front door opens and she shouts out. They hear Morgan calling her to the kitchen and the door closing behind her. Morgan had been insistent that Bray and Gavan keep out of the way while he speaks to her.

Garvan rests against the sill and crosses his arms. 'So, do you trust her?'

Bray makes a face. 'I haven't seen her for over twelve years. We used to be close.' Bray shrugs. 'If she's Foundation military, she's not going to be too keen on having a Hunter and an ex-prisoner staying with her dad—relation or not.'

'Erin! Stop! Just wait!' Morgan shouts from downstairs.

Heavy footsteps race up the stairs. Bray and

Garvan tense as the door to Bray's room slams back. 'Leave this to me,' Bray mutters before the door to the room they're in crashes open. Erin stands in the doorway and glowers at her younger cousin. Bray tries to hold his ground but Erin has always had a strange way of unnerving him.

'So, it's true. I thought Dad might have been helping himself to more than his share of scotch.'

'Hi Erin.'

She crosses her arms over her chest, hiding the Foundation logo on the breast of her jacket. 'Hi? Are you serious? You can't just waltz back in here with a hi after all this time. Do you have any idea what Mum and Dad went through when you left Vana without an explanation? You just vanished.'

Bray spins away from her. 'Not now, Erin.' He barely stops himself from tumbling through the glass as Erin shoves him from behind. 'Don't brush me off.'

In that instant, Bray is pulled back into his childhood. Endless stupid arguments over equally stupid things. Without thinking, he shoves her back.

Garvan steps in between the cousins. 'How about you guys kiss and make up instead.'

'Tell your boyfriend to back off,' Erin growls at Bray.

Garvan takes a few steps back. 'Backing off.'

Bray jams a finger in Erin's shoulder. 'Hey, don't take out your bad mood on him.'

Erin jabs him back, a little harder than Bray had.

'Bad mood? Are you kidding me? This is about you

cutting us out of your life.'

'Funny, I distinctly remember being the one in the back of the security transport on my way to Vana. Leaving wasn't my choice.'

'Cutting off all contact with us was. Nan and Grandpa supported you and you just upped and left without a word. The next thing we hear you're the latest inmate in Tyrat.'

'I don't need you to go through my backstory. I was there.'

'But you didn't think for one minute that anyone in the family would want to know—did you? No, as usual, you shut us all out and dealt with it alone.'

Bray snorts. 'It's not like I had much choice. They're not too keen on having visitors for tea and cakes at Tyrat.'

Erin waves her arms in the air. 'There you go again. Are you ever going to take things seriously?'

'My life was on the line every day in that place. I took that damn seriously.'

'You didn't have to be there. Don't you get that? If your family knew what was happening, we might have been able to help.'

Bray leans closer to Erin, stopping with his nose a hairs width from hers. 'Tyrat is a one-way deal. Everyone knows that.'

Her smile is far from pleasant. 'Yet, here you are. How did you get out?'

Bray steps back, shaking his head in anger. 'Why? You want to run back to your Foundation mates with the intel? Figure out a way to stop any more innocent inmates from getting their life back?'

Erin laughs harshly. 'Innocent, really? So the charges brought against you for smuggling and murder, they were made up?'

Bray doesn't respond.

'Didn't think so.'

With neither side likely to back down, Bray fully expects this to get physical. Before they can take the argument further, firm hands haul Bray away and wrap around his torso. He struggles against the hold on him but Garvan won't budge. As Garvan struggles to keep control of Bray, Morgan deals with his daughter.

Even though he's shorter than Erin, Morgan manages to keep her at bay. 'What the hell are you two playing at? If the neighbours hear you two eejits we're all in a mound of trouble.'

Bray shoves Garvan aside and faces Morgan. 'Just working some things out.'

'Is that right?' Morgan glares at Bray. 'I expect this from you, but Erin, you're a Foundation officer. You should know better.'

Bray laughs harshly, wincing as his bruised ribs protest. 'Sorry Morgan, guess I led her astray, again.'

'Enough!' Morgan's sudden outburst silences any further argument. 'I don't want to hear another word from either of you. You're family. Shayla would be horrified at the two of you.'

Morgan points towards the door. 'Downstairs.

Both of you.' Without argument, Bray and Erin trudge ahead of Morgan down the stairs and into the kitchen. Morgan slams the door behind them then points to the large kitchen table. 'Sit.'

Knowing better than to argue with him when he's in this mood, the cousins do as they're told. Erin and Bray sit at either end as far from each other as possible. Morgan sits to one side but Garvan remains standing.

'This is clearly a family thing. I might just take myself out of the equation.'

Morgan nods briskly, allowing Garvan to make a swift, tactical retreat. Bray barely resists the urge to race after him. He's going to have a serious word with him about abandoning a fellow Hunter when he's up to his neck in trouble.

Morgan takes a deep breath before speaking, 'If I ever see that kind of behaviour from either of you again, I will personally make your lives a living hell. Do you both understand?'

Erin opens her mouth to speak but Morgan silences her by thumping his fist against the table-top. 'Do you understand, Erin?'

She clenches her jaw as she looks away. She finally nods once. Morgan turns his attention to Bray. 'Brayden?'

'I understand.'

'Good. That's a start. Erin, I've said that Bray and Garvan can stay here until they figure out a way to get back to the Outer Sector.'

She takes off her jacket and drapes it on the back of her chair. 'That's a mistake. If the Foundation find out you're harbouring fugitives, they'll ship you off to the nearest prison. If Bray has any sense left, he'll take his boyfriend and leave immediately.'

'I'm not going to just kick him out. Your mother wouldn't be impressed with me if I did.'

'Yeah, well she's not here to take the fall with you.'

Morgan glances at his daughter. Something passes between them and Bray feels like he's intruding in a personal grief. Bray clears his throat. 'The last thing we want is to cause problems. We have nowhere else to go.'

Erin's head snaps around to look at Bray. 'You could have stayed the hell away.' She shakes her head and laughs abruptly. 'I'm a Foundation officer. My job, my life is on the line too. I have to report this.'

'Please, Erin. give us time to figure out a way off Earth. I know we're asking a lot but please keep this to yourself.'

She stands up and shuffles to the window. Her shoulders rise and drop as she takes a deep breath. 'Damn it. Fine.'

'Thanks,' Bray mutters.

She spins to look down at him. 'I'm not doing this for you. You've landed my family in shit again. I'll keep quiet for Dad, but I do have a condition.'

'What?' Bray asks, feeling a little wary.

'I want to talk to you alone.'

Morgan shakes his head. 'Erin...'

'I'm not going to beat him up. He's in enough trouble as it is. I just want a quick word in private.' Morgan quietly, yet reluctantly leaves the room and shuts the door behind him. Once alone, Erin settles back in the chair and examines Bray.

Without being too obvious, Bray gets a proper look at his cousin. The meek, scrawny girl has grown into an impressive woman. Her shoulder length dark hair is secured in a tail at the base of her neck, a few locks have escaped after their disagreement. Her piercing blue eyes are cold and seem to constantly be taking in her surroundings. The Foundation issue shirt hides a toned body. After what he just experienced with her, she'd be more than capable of holding her own in any Hunter training room. She may even give Garvan a run for his money. The gold insignia on her top surprises Bray. She's a Commander. He knows enough about the Foundation to know that's no mean feat. Although the Foundation prided themselves on offering both sexes the same opportunities, women still struggled to gain any positions of importance in the HQ. If Erin is actually a Commander, she's one formidable woman.

She leans back in her chair and raises a dark eyebrow. 'Quit staring and let me see them.'

'See what?'

'Your marks.'

Bray considers refusing, but he needs to keep her on his side—for the moment at least. He takes off his jacket and throws it onto the chair beside him. Her eyes narrow as she closely examines the tattoo.

'Hunter or Nomad?'

Bray frowns and stares at her. 'You know about the groups?'

She nods. 'Enough to know you're one of them.'

'Hunter.'

Erin nods slowly. 'Just great,' she mutters under her breath. 'What's your rank?'

'What the hell does that have to do with anything?'

'One call and you're on a transport back to prison. Don't mess with me, Bray. Answer the question.'

'Commander.'

She curses and pushes back from the table. 'You have got to be kidding me.'

'What about you?' Bray knows the answer, but wants the kick of hearing her say it.

Erin frowns. 'Me what?'

'Rank.'

'Same,' she mutters quietly.

Bray can't help the smile that breaks free at her confirmation. Even after all the bad choices he's made, he's still reached the exact same rank as his perfect cousin. 'Bet that hurts.'

She clenches her fists on the table. 'At least I'm not a smuggler, a thief, a murderer, and an escaped prisoner.'

Bray smirks and nods. 'Impressive list of achievements when you say it like that.'

Her eyes harden. 'How did you get here in the first place?'

'Hitched a ride on a recycling unit from the HQ.'

She sighs. 'Not the house. I meant how did you get to Earth. The Hunters are based in the Outer Sector, right?'

'We got stuck on *Alpha* when she was in the Outer Sector. Before we knew what was happening, she was on her way here.'

She frowns. '*Alpha*? You sure about that?'

Bray nods. 'I'm sure. Why?'

'*Alpha* is reserved for Council use only. I'm surprised you were able to get on board. She should have been secured against unwelcome intruders.' She picks at a groove in the table. 'Who knows you're on the surface?'

'No one spotted us in the base.' Bray pauses unsure whether to mention the surprise they left in the wall.

Erin's eyes narrow. 'What?'

'We had to... borrow a couple of hands.'

She frowns for a moment then her eyebrows shoot up as she realises what Bray is saying. 'Let me get this straight. You arrive on Earth in secret and to keep your presence here under wraps, you and your mate separate two crew members from their hands. Are they going to be looking for said hands back?'

Bray grimaces and shakes his head.'

'Just perfect. Thanks a lot.' She rubs a hand across her forehead. 'Right. I know I'm going to regret asking, but what happened to the owners of the hands?'

'We put them behind a wall panel in a storage room on *Alpha*. They're with the body of a cyborg Garvan killed en route.'

She openly stares at him. 'Oh, that's just great. Anything else I should know about? Any more bodies or body parts scattered over the fields on the way here?'

'What the hell does it matter to you?'

She gets up and leans over him. 'It matters to me because, at the moment, I'm the only thing separating you from a cosy cell in Tyrat.' She takes her jacket off the chair and shrugs it on as she strides towards the door. 'Tell Dad I'll see him later.'

'Where are you going?'

'Back to work. Relax,' she says when Bray gets to his feet, 'I have to check if you idiots have been noticed yet. I'm not going to do anything to jeopardise my dad. Unfortunately, that means keeping my mouth shut about you two and masking any tracks you may have left.' She stands in front of Bray, her eyes meeting his. 'If you do anything to put him at risk, I'll bring you in myself—cousin or not.' With a last exasperated look over her shoulder, she opens the back door.

'Hang on, you have access to *Alpha*?'

Erin's blue eyes seem to darken as she glares at him. 'Of course I do. I'm the head of security.'

Bray's skin tingles at her announcement. 'You are?'

She nods once. 'That's right. Why do you think I'm

so happy to see you here,' she replies sarcastically. 'If the Council learns that I'm helping you, my punishment will be instant death. I know too much to be allowed to live. By coming back from the dead, you've put my neck on the block, literally. By the way, aerial drones do a fly by every now and again. I'll get the schedule and send it through to Dad. Until I do that, you two keep out of sight.'

Bray slumps back in to his chair as Erin shuts the door a little harder than necessary. This family reunion is going as badly as he imagined it would.

'Sir, we have the footage from the cargo hold.'

One ignores Leeson for another few minutes, but not because he's busy. He likes to keep the man waiting. In fact, he likes to keep everyone waiting. If he dropped everything when a subordinate came to see him, it would give his visitor ideas above their station. After ignoring Leeson for six minutes, he slowly looks up from his screen. 'What are you waiting for? Show me.'

Leeson snaps to attention and places the monitor on the table in front of him. One reaches across and takes it, then leans back in his plush chair to examine the data.

'Did you unearth anything?'

'The recording is set up at the relevant section.'

One activates the recording. He can't stop the sneer that pulls at his lip when he sees two men step off the ramp. They may be in Foundation uniforms but he can tell they don't belong. The larger of the two men glances around the room and One's stomach drops when he looks at the camera. He rewinds and replays the footage again, pausing when the man looks directly at the screen. He zooms in for a better look and the pad drops to the table.

'Is everything all right, sir?'

'Search *Alpha*. I want every square inch of her examined. Pull off each and every panel and remove the floors. I don't care what you do to the ship. Find out what he did when he was on board.'

'Sir?'

'You have your orders. Now leave.'

'But, sir—'

'I said leave!'

One stares in horror at the screen in front of him as Leeson scurries from the room. Once the door is secured, he searches his bottom drawer and pulls out a small unregistered and completely untraceable unit. He requests the prison records from Tyrat and scrolls through the list of names until he locates the right one. Wade Garvan is listed, but it's the text beside the man's name that radiates a cold chill up his spine. It appears Wade was one of the prisoners the rebels took when they attacked the prison.

One gets to his feet and paces the thick carpet in front of the large expanse of shielded glass serving as a wall of his office. When he put Wade Garvan in Tyrat, he assumed he'd never hear the man's name again. He'd get lost in the system, or die. Either way, his problems would disappear along with him.

He never expected to see him again, let alone have him appear in the cargo bay stepping off *Alpha*. Of all the people to be reunited with, Wade was well below the bottom of his list. Having him on Earth is too close for comfort. Having him alive is pushing it.

One glances back at the screen on his desk. Wade Garvan can tear his world apart if he wants to. One's fists clench at his sides. Well, there's no way he's going to allow that to happen. He spent too long working up to this position. He won't let a convict bring it all crashing down around him.

This time he'll just have to make sure Wade dies, even if that means killing him personally.

∞

Bray launches the bale of hay across the floor and up to the mezzanine level of the hay barn. He wipes a dusty arm across his sweat-soaked forehead and looks around the building. Morgan clearly hasn't lost his dislike of technology. He should have more than enough income to support the use of drones on the farm, but looking around, he can't see that anything has been upgraded since he left over a decade ago.

Bray wouldn't be surprised if this were the only farm left on the planet that didn't have a full drone workforce to take care of all the manual labour.

He picks up another bale and tosses it above his head. He inhales a cloud of hay dust and sneezes. Then again, he can't imagine anything better than getting your hands dirty on the land—even if it does make you sneeze.

'Still allergic to hay, huh?'

Bray looks over his shoulder as Erin steps around the doorframe. She leans against the support pillar and crosses her arms. Her dark hair is loose and hiding her cold eyes.

'You don't tend to come across much hay on a ship.' Bray dusts off his hands. 'Well?'

'You're in the clear.'

'You sure?'

She snorts and nods once. 'Of course I'm sure. You really think I'm going to do a half-assed check? I don't give a damn about you and your mate, but my dad and I are a very different matter. I'm sure you're clear... for now anyway. There's nothing to say that's still the case at this moment.'

Bray turns his back to her and resumes his work. 'If you have any bright ideas on how to get us back to the Outer Sector, I'm all ears.'

Erin scales the ladder and hauls two of the bales over to the corner above Bray. 'If I could shove you both on the first transport off Earth, you'd be on it. Problem we have is that the Foundation scan every square inch of everything leaving the surface.'

'Bit paranoid.'

'That's nothing. The checks are carried out again as they enter the Port. Anything suspicious results in the ship not materialising on the other side.'

Bray openly stares at his cousin. 'You serious?'

She steps out of the way as Bray throws another bale onto the upper level. Erin drags it over to the pile in the corner. 'Not something I'd joke about. We take security seriously.'

'We?'

She peers down at him. 'Yes, we.' Bray snorts. Erin launches a rag at Bray's head. 'Don't piss me off, Bray. It's only a matter of time before the bodies are found. You're going to need me to give you a head's up. Wouldn't want me to forget.'

Bray mock salutes and drops down onto a bale. 'Hey, if ships are that closely monitored, how did *Alpha* get through with me and Garvan on board?'

Erin delays answering until she's climbed down the ladder. 'Good question. Maybe she's not as well checked as the other ships. There's a hell of a lot of privacy and secrecy surrounding the Council. Only staff handpicked by One are allowed on the ship. I have access to her on the surface, but once she leaves, all my people have to be clear.'

Bray nods. Too much about being on Earth is a foreign concept. He feels completely out of his depth. He's hating every second of having his life in someone else's hands. At the moment, there's not a lot else he can do though.

He glances up as she lowers onto the bale beside him. 'Where were you all these years?' Erin asks.

Bray makes a face. 'Probably best you don't know.'

'Worse than Tyrat?'

'It's a long story and I'm not in the mood for sharing right now.'

She nods. 'Your decision. Listen, I may be angry as hell at you for putting my dad in this situation, but I guess we're still family.' Erin looks towards the field outside the large double doors. 'You can trust us, Bray. You can trust me.'

Bray forces what he hopes is a convincing smile on his face. 'Thanks, but I'll pass for now.'

She sighs. 'Whatever. Suit yourself.'

Erin shoves the barn door back with her foot and leaves Bray alone. Bray pushes to his feet and gets back to work. He seriously doubts he'll ever be able to open up about his messed up life.

∞

'Did he say anything to you?'

Erin slumps into the seat beside her dad and shakes her head. 'Nothing about where he's been. In typical Bray fashion, he's keeping it to himself.'

Morgan takes a sip of his steaming coffee and is quiet for a moment. 'What the hell are those... things on him?'

She takes a deep breath as she stares into the

murky depths of her own drink. 'I have no idea, Dad. I've never seen anything like it before. Whatever is on his chest is fused to his skin.' She runs a hand through her hair and looks over to Morgan. 'I do recognise the tattoos, however. I questioned him and he admitted he's a Commander on a Hunter ship.'

'As in the Outer Sector Hunters? I've only heard bad things about them.'

'That's putting it mildly. There are two main groups on our radar—the Hunters and the Nomad. The Nomad are the main concern, no doubt, but that doesn't mean the Hunters are a fleet of angels. If the Foundation figure out he's here, they'll come after him. No question about it.'

'And...'

'And, well, let's just say we'd never see Bray again.'

Morgan massages the back of his neck then shoves back from the table. 'He let it slip that he's been tortured.' Erin curses under her breath. 'He may be a transport load of trouble, but he's Maggie's son. I can't kick him out after thinking he was dead for so long.'

'I understand, but he needs to tell us what happened to him. If he's going to be staying here, I need all the details. At least that way I can know what to plan for.'

Morgan snorts. 'I agree, but you know what Bray's like, he'll only talk when he's good and ready and not a minute before. Pushing him will only reinforce his wall.'

Morgan gets to his feet and disappears into the living room, returning a few minutes later with a bottle of scotch in his hands. He takes a glass out of the cupboard beside him and pours a measure.

'Dad, you only have two measures left for the rest of the month.'

'The Foundation's alcohol quota is the least of my concerns right now. We buried him, Erin. Well... you know what I mean. He was dead.'

She nods. 'I know, and I want to know where he's been just as much as you do. I just can't see him opening up any time soon. Unfortunately, time isn't our friend. There's bound to be some record somewhere of his arrival, whether he hid his presence or not. The Foundation will realise he's here. When that happens we're all in trouble. This is the first place they'll come looking for him.'

'No, it's not.'

Erin looks up at Bray's unexpected appearance and frowns. 'Yes actually, it is.'

Bray leans back against the sink and crosses his arms. 'It's a long story but I'm not linked to this family anymore.'

Morgan laughs. 'Don't be ridiculous.'

'I mean it. Someone I worked with had the power to alter Foundation records. I'm no longer listed at this residence or as being related to you. You're safe.'

Morgan jumps to his feet and slams the glass down on the wooden table-top. 'Let me get this straight. You wiped us from your record?'

'I was wiped from your records to be exact.'

'Well that's just perfect. You weren't content to die, you had to erase yourself from the family altogether.'

'Morgan, it's not like that. It was done for your safety.'

Morgan looks up at Bray, but doesn't fully recognise the young man in front of him. For years he wished things had been different, wished that Bray and Daegan were alive and living on the farm with Shayla and Erin, but every morning he woke up to the same chilling reality. Maggie, Shayla, Daegan, and Bray were gone and there wasn't a damn thing he could do about it.

Now, faced with one of his dreams come true, he's not sure exactly what his wish has brought to life. The skin against the strange metal on Bray's face crinkles as his nephew frowns at him. Bray's strange, mismatched eyes examine him. There's too much about Bray he doesn't understand. The young, strong-willed, argumentative, stubborn man has turned into... whatever he is. He doesn't understand the changes Bray made to himself and he's not sure he wants to know.

'Are you going to give us any more information or do you expect us to blindly accept the little snippets you decide to feed us?'

'You're just going to have to trust me.'

Morgan sneers, 'Then I guess we're in trouble, aren't we?'

Bray nods slowly. 'I guess we are.'

'Think you'll get her going?'

Bray doesn't look up at Morgan as he examines the engine. 'Not ready to give up on her.'

Morgan saunters around the old transport and settles on a bale of hay. He stretches his legs out in front of him and silently watches Bray work. Bray does his best to ignore his uncle as he battles with the transport engine. He'd won the run down Series-1 transport at an illegal game of poker when he was in school, but as far as Morgan was concerned, Bray bought it from the re-cycler before it was made into a new transport. Like most things between him and Morgan, the transport became the source of many arguments. Morgan wanted him to stop wasting his time and scrap it, but Bray, being stubborn and always needing to do the exact opposite of what Morgan said, kept it and continued to work on it.

Hopefully, with the new parts Erin is getting, she'll make it off the ground again.

'Is that what you think I've done with you?' Bray looks up, frowning. 'Given up on you,' Morgan explains.

Bray goes back to the engine. 'I'm a little busy here.'

'You do think that, don't you?'

Bray thumps the wrench against the engine. 'I really have to get this done. We need to get out of here ASAP. Erin's neck is on the line the longer we stay here.'

Morgan shakes his head. 'She knows what she's doing. In spite of her initial reaction, she wants to help you. You didn't twist her arm.' Morgan smiles. 'Then again, you never had to twist her arm.'

Bray looks over his shoulder at Morgan. 'I thought you always blamed me for getting her into trouble?'

Morgan laughs and shakes his head. 'You were both as much trouble as each other.'

'Then why did you send me away?'

Morgan gets to his feet and leans against the side of the transport. 'I was terrified you'd come back to us in a body-bag.'

'What?'

'You were getting in deeper and deeper with the

wrong people. If I'm being honest, I was relieved when I heard you were in prison—better than the alternative. At the time, I thought sending you to Vana would save you, take you off whatever destructive path you were stuck on.' Morgan shrugs. 'Seems I was wrong. It only gave you an easier way out. Maggie would kick my ass if she knew how badly I'd messed up with you.'

Bray snorts and shakes his head.

Morgan narrows his eyes as he examines Bray. 'Shayla said something to me after you left. I always thought she was seeing something that wasn't there, but now I'm not so sure.'

'Yeah, and what's that?'

'She told me you thought Maggie and Dean didn't care about you. I thought she had it wrong, but she didn't.'

Bray pauses before getting himself together again. 'It was a long time ago. Can we just forget it?'

Morgan takes Bray's arm, forcing him to stop working. 'Brayden, you and your brother were their whole world. After Daegan... they tried to keep things as normal for you as they could, that's why you spent so much time here.'

'You don't have to do this. It's fine, really.'

'No. You need to listen to me. For the first time in your life, you will listen to me. One half of their world disappeared along with Daegan—one half. They never brushed you aside, never forgot about you, not once. They wanted the best life possible for you.'

'Just not with them, right?'

Morgan curses and looks up at the ceiling, muttering under his breath. He takes a long, deep breath before looking back at him. 'Bray, Maggie and Dean couldn't live on Earth. They weren't allowed to.'

'Why not?'

'Foundation rules. Dean wasn't Daegan's father. The fact that Maggie got pregnant out of marriage at such a young age meant she went against Foundation law.' He curses loudly. 'Damn Foundation and their rules. She didn't have a choice but to leave. Dean married her, but the damage to her reputation was done, so he took his new wife and they left for Vana. Life was hard for them. Vana isn't affluent, as you know, and she felt Daegan and you weren't having as good a start in life as she wanted. It wasn't ideal, but she came back to Earth, under the radar of course, listing you and Daegan as being under my guardianship. You both attended Foundation schools and had the life she wanted for you. Unfortunately, Maggie and Dean had to return to Vana regularly to at least pretend they lived there. They needed to keep as much attention off you boys as possible.'

'You're kidding, right?'

Instead of answering, Morgan pulls the side off one of the support beams at the back of the barn to uncover a small keypad. He punches in a code, exposing a large trapdoor in the floor. He steps aside and nods to Bray. 'Take a look for yourself.'

Curiosity gets the better of Bray. He gets to his feet

and approaches the large hole in the floor. Polished wooden steps descend into a brightly light room. He freezes at the bottom as images from his past rush back into his mind. He remembers being in here before. The underground room takes up the entire floor space of the barn above. He wanders through the living area and into the kitchenette. He runs his hand over the smooth worktop, his fingers tracing the perfect circle burnt into the wood.

'I left the heating coil from your tractor on the surface.'

Morgan laughs. 'Maggie was as angry at me as she was at you about that.'

Bray looks towards the three doors in the far wall. Instinct leads him to the room at the far left. He opens the door, smiling when he notices the set of bunk beds against the wall. Morgan stops just behind him and looks into the room. 'Seems even back then you were set for a life in space.'

Bray looks at the spaceship themed sheets on the bottom bunk. His old bed. Gryffin's top bunk had pirates on it. Appropriate for both of them. 'He wanted the bottom bunk.'

Morgan nods. 'You weren't having any of it. You kept complaining that you'd fall off. You were never too keen on heights.'

'In the end he gave in though.'

'He let you have your way more times than you probably remember.'

Bray slowly lowers onto his bunk. 'How have I

forgotten all this?'

Morgan sits on the chair opposite him. 'Sounds like you've had enough to occupy your mind since you left. Besides, your parents never wanted this to be the norm for you. You only came down here for a treat every now and again. This was the only way they could be here with you. In those days things were a little more relaxed. There were no drones to patrol the area. If any patrols came by, your parents would come down here. The floor is shielded so there's nothing to attract any attention.'

Bray feels like a transport has hit him full force in the chest. He now realises what his parents had gone through to make sure he had a good life. After Daegan disappeared he focused on the fact they seemed to be more interested in finding Daegan than in spending time with him. 'They did so much for us. All this was so we could have a better life, and I just threw it all away. I did exactly what she didn't want me to do.'

Morgan crouches down in front of him. 'No. All they wanted was for you and Daegan to be happy. Are you happy?'

Bray frowns. 'Apart from my current predicament, yes.'

Morgan shrugs. 'There are you. Maggie and Dean would be happy as long as you are. She loved you so damn much, son. They both did. I can honestly say she'd be so proud of you, Brayden.' Morgan glances down at the tattoos on his arms. 'In spite of your best efforts.'

Morgan slaps him on the shoulder and helps him up. 'Whatever you've done or whoever you are now... I know Maggie would have accepted you.' Morgan shakes his head and smiles. 'Knowing her, she probably would have wanted to see the Outer Sector. Never could keep that girl out of trouble.'

Bray nods slowly as he looks around his old home. 'You know, it's probably best if Garvan and I bunk down here... if that's okay with you.'

'You don't need to do that. Erin knows when the aerial drones are scheduled to do their passes. We'll just make sure you're hidden before they come around.'

Bray smiles at the various brightly coloured drawings stuck to the front of the fridge. 'No. I think it's best we're out of the way. We'll stick to the barn and the house for meals.'

Morgan nods. 'You're probably right. No point taking chances.' He strolls to the door and looks back at Bray. 'How about we stop talking and get this pile of junk you won off the ground.'

Bray's face drops at Morgan's words. 'What?'

Morgan laughs and shakes his head. 'Found it? Seriously, Bray, you couldn't come up with something better than that?'

'How long have you known?'

'Since the day you came home with it on the back of a transport.'

'B-but why didn't you say anything?'

Morgan glances over his shoulder as he mounts the stairs. 'Why would I? You were so pleased with yourself for getting one over on me. I couldn't ruin it for you. Now, would you stop catching flies and help me repair your ship.'

∞

Bray shovels another forkful of food into his mouth. He glances across at Garvan and manages to keep the rice in his mouth when he sees the man inhale the food like he's never eaten before. He swallows and laughs. 'You're not in prison anymore. You can take a breath between mouthfuls.'

Garvan grins around a very full mouth. After a few more chews, he swallows and smiles apologetically at Morgan and Erin. 'Sorry about that. The food is just so good.'

Erin laughs. 'You go for it.'

Morgan grunts. 'Anything's good compared to prison food.'

'Any more comments like that and you can cook your own dinner, Dad.' Erin looks down at her comms unit and excuses herself from the table.

Bray smiles as he watches the interaction around the table. Hunter meals were usually chaotic, with everyone eating fast and running to get back to their stations. He'd forgotten what being part of a family dinner was like. Even with the large hole left by Shayla, Erin and Morgan seem to be as strong as ever.

Morgan knocks on the table in front of him. 'What are you grinning about?'

'I guess I just missed this.'

'Yeah well, enjoy it while you can.' Bray looks up to see Erin standing in the doorway. She throws her personal unit on the table, barely missing the bowl of rice.

'Hey,' Morgan snaps. 'What's wrong with you?'

She paces beside the door, her hands resting on her hips. 'Read it.'

Morgan reaches out and scans through the data. He passes the unit to Garvan. 'Care to shed some light on this?'

Bray gets up to read the report over Garvan's shoulder. 'Wade Garvan. Escaped prisoner. Armed and extremely dangerous. Use caution when apprehending. Reward offered for his capture.' Bray sits back down and looks over at Garvan. 'Who have you ticked off?'

Garvan shrugs. 'I guess my reputation precedes me. Where's this notice posted?'

Erin slumps into the nearest chair. 'Security personnel only. The Council doesn't want your escape becoming public knowledge.'

'Should I be flattered by the reward?'

'Five million credits.'

Garvan's eyebrows shoot up. 'It seems so.'

Morgan takes the unit from Garvan. 'What does this mean for us?'

She makes a face. 'There's still nothing to point to them being here. I don't think it affects anything right now, but everyone with a weapon will be keeping an eye out for him. He's too hot to leave the property.'

'Now you're embarrassing me, Commander.'

Erin sighs and shakes her head. 'Glad you can still laugh about it. If you're found, you won't be doing much laughing.'

Garvan stands up and shoves his hands in his pockets. 'I don't doubt that. If you'll excuse me, I think I need a little air... while I can still get it.'

Erin waits until Garvan has left before she leans forward to talk to Bray. 'He's hiding something.'

'Like what?'

'How the hell am I supposed to know? This order came from high up, Bray. It's serious.'

'We've managed to piss off quite a few people lately. That put everyone in our group on the wanted list.'

'You must have shown up on one of the base security cameras. I thought you said you were careful?'

'Have you been in the hangar? There are cameras everywhere. You'd swear the Foundation has a trust issue. I'm not surprised one of us got caught. The Council probably just has its nose out of joint because we're here in the first place.'

Erin shakes her head briskly, loosening some strands from their tie. 'It's a lot more than that. This order personally came from One.'

Morgan sits up straight. 'Are you sure?'

She nods. 'Usually the Council or their subordinates look after things like this. For One to issue the order, well, your friend must have done something to really get in his bad books.'

Bray looks out the back door after Garvan. He has a horrible feeling their situation just took a leap up the trouble scale.

Bray wanders around the side of the house, down the dirt track leading to the barn, and through the trapdoor in the floor. He finds Garvan leaning against the sink, his hands clenching the counter-top behind him. 'What's going on, Garvan?'

The other man frowns as he looks down at his boots. 'You know as much as I do, Commander.'

Bray clasps his hands in front of him. 'Why don't I believe you?'

Garvan laughs. 'That's rich coming from you.'

'What does that mean?'

'You've been economical with the truth since we got to this blasted planet.'

'They've got enough to deal with without adding my colourful past to the mix.'

Garvan turns to face him. 'I don't mean that and you know it. Your family are mourning someone who's still alive. And before you say anything, the cyborg issue is bull. You said it yourself, you may not have been the good little boy they wanted, but they're putting their necks on the line to keep us safe. Doesn't strike me as the actions of people who are disgusted or disappointed in what you are, not that they fully understand because you haven't told them.'

'I've already warned you to butt out of this. What the hell is your problem?'

Garvan pokes a finger in Bray's chest, forcing him to take a step back. 'You're the damn problem, Commander. All you've done since we got here is make excuses. You won't talk about Gryffin, won't talk about your implants, won't trust your family with the truth, and even though you want to take down the Foundation, you've done nothing about it.'

'In case you haven't noticed, we're trapped on Earth with no ship. What do you expect me to do? Launch a full scale attack on Council HQ from the back of a cow!'

'There you go again with your excuses. There's a hell of a lot you can do. For starters, your cousin is the head of Foundation security. Use her.'

'How?'

Garvan looks away, shaking his head. 'Figure it out. Why don't you start by telling them the truth about what the Foundation are doing? Do you really think Erin would sit back and do nothing if she knew what happened to you and Gryffin?'

'Yeah, right. It's not that simple. There's no way either of them would believe a word of it. I don't believe it and I've witnessed it first-hand. Knowing what happened to me won't do anything to improve Erin and Morgan's life. Besides, I'm not sure I want to tell them.'

'Oh poor you. You know what? I'm beginning to understand why your parents named you after the noise a jackass makes.'

Bray's mouth drops as he looks at Garvan. 'What the hell did you say?'

'You heard me. Being on Earth isn't just tough on you. I've got a past I'd prefer not to bump into. At least you can sort yours out easily. Stop using who you are and who Gryffin is to avoid growing a set and telling them the truth. After everything they've done for us, it's the least they deserve.'

'Oh, it's that simple, huh?'

'Well, it's not the mammoth task you've made it out to be in your head.'

Bray steps up to Garvan. 'Fine, I'll talk to them if you tell me what the hell is going on between you and One.'

Garvan snorts. 'Of course you will.'

'I give you my word. Why is One after you?'

Garvan looks back towards the ground and is quiet for a long time. 'You back out of this, I'm not going to be too happy with you.'

'Understood.'

'Fine. I'm a threat to his perfect little existence.'

'What do you mean?'

Garvan squeezes his eyes shut. He shakes his head, then opens his eyes again. 'I'm an escaped prisoner. Not the best advertisement for a no second chances government.'

'It's more than that.' Bray sits on the counter beside Garvan. 'I know I've got a lot to talk about with my family. I get it, okay.' He takes a deep breath, not looking forward to getting personal with Garvan. 'Since I met you, I've felt close to you.'

Garvan tilts his head to look at Bray and raises one eyebrow.

Bray thumps him in the arm. 'Not like that.'

'That's a relief.'

'I mean that I trust you. You've been there for me when you could easily have just walked away. You're a Hunter, Garvan. That's a given.'

Garvan smirks, but doesn't respond.

'Hunters look out for each other. We're family. Tell me what's going on. Let me help.'

Garvan shakes his head. 'Nothing you can do to help. Nothing anyone can do. He's the head of the Council and I'm...' He sighs. 'Well, on Earth, I'm nothing... not anymore.'

Bray studies the large man. Whatever is going on between Garvan and One, he gets the feeling it's personal. He's never seen Garvan look so lost. It's like the mention of the man sapped all his life away. 'Is this about your work on the new colony?'

Garvan laughs harshly. 'That was just the carrot he used to capture me.'

'Capture you? I don't understand. What the hell did he do to you?'

Bray is just about to give up on getting any response when Garvan finally speaks. 'He destroyed my parents, my family, and me just to keep his dirty little secret safe.'

∞

One waits until the lift door seals before he places his palm against the scanner. Once the system recognises him, a secondary panel slides out from the wall. Only the Council have access to the private elevators that run the length and width of the HQ and main hangar. Nothing adds to the mystery of the Council more than appearing unannounced when people least expect it.

He chooses the correct floor and clasps his hands in front of him as the lift silently ferries him to his destination. The lift drops into the main hanger, entering *Alpha* through a port attached to her top deck. Without the slightest movement, the lift arrives and the doors open. He steps out into his private office on board *Alpha*.

Like his office in the HQ building, his quarters on board are just as opulent, if not a bit smaller.

Initially, he wanted to take the entire deck for his personal space, but the designers and his fellow Council members were not eager to oblige. He'd already taken ten of the lower decks away, *Alpha* couldn't afford to lose any more space. He had conceded, although he was less than happy about it.

He gathers the file of new door codes from his desk before stepping back into the lift and dropping to the lower decks. Instead of the opulence of the upper levels, stark metal walls and floors greet him. His thick, red robe brushes against the rough floor as he marches along the corridor. He presses his hand to the panel outside the fifth door and keys in the newly altered code. The doors part to show a tiered viewing area with a glass wall opposite. He strides over to the wall and peers down into the newly built lab.

When the Council decided to bring cyborg production back from the Outer Sector, they thought it best to have the site portable. After what happened to the new colony, One is glad they did. If HQ was ever compromised—not that it ever would be—the Council would just have to board *Alpha*, and take the entire production line with them. It was One's idea and one that he is proud of. Having the lab on *Alpha* also means there is no chance of it being accidentally discovered. Only One, the Council, and the doctors have access.

One examines the scene below him. A team of Foundation doctors and engineers are gathered around a screen at the far side of the laboratory. He climbs down the metal stairs and steps through the door at the bottom. As soon as the locks disengage, the team spins around and bows. The senior doctor hurries over and bows again. 'Sir, it's a pleasure to see you.'

One ignores the pitiful grovelling and strides over to the holding cell behind the nervous team. He clasps his hands behind his back and looks at the young woman strapped to the table in the centre of the room. 'How is she?'

The senior doctor nods enthusiastically. 'She's performing better than we expected. It seems our theory was correct.'

One smiles. The retched Scientist had been so wrapped up with trying to save the woman he carried around with him, that it took him longer to see what the Foundation doctors were quick to discover. Millions of credits and hundreds of test subjects were wasted thanks to a glaring oversight on behalf of the Scientist. The prototype was a complete fluke. There was nothing more to it than that. The flaw that was killing all the subjects came down to gender. For some reason, they died because they were male. Once the Foundation doctors figured this out and began testing the theory, the tables turned.

The woman was the first of many to be tested and so far, all have survived. The female prototype was fitted with the new improved control implant last week with another fourteen since then. 'Is she accepting commands?'

'Yes, sir. As you ordered, we have kept her design similar to that of the original prototype. Her mods are more advanced but operate as his do. We fitted the artificial arm yesterday. The programming is accepting the new limb, but she will need a few days to fully become accustomed to it.'

'Good.' While personal vendetta's stifled the Scientists potential, there was no denying he had created an impressive prototype. Apart from some programming flaws the Foundation quickly rectified, they were able to utilise the majority of the man's work. Strength, endurance, and obedience could be programmed and that was the most important thing. The doctors were also able to shut off all pain receptors. The new batch of cyborgs will keep going at full strength until they shut down. In truth, it was better than One had planned for. Once the testing stage is completed, they can go into mass production, taking women from wherever they have to and build his army.

If everything goes to plan, they can have hundreds of the soldiers on a transport to the Outer Sector within a few weeks. With an army like that fighting for them, the colonists would be unable to defend themselves. After the colonists were subdued, the Foundation could take over, put the colonists to work and commence shipping resources and raw materials back to Earth.

'Keep me up to date with your progress.'

The doctor nods, then looks down at his tablet.

'Sir, testing is going well, but progress would be sped up if we had access to the male prototype.'

One clenches his jaw but recovers quickly. 'I understand, Doctor, but for now, he must remain where he is. You'll have to make do with the vast pool of resources I've made available to you.'

The doctor nods quickly and bows again. One resists the urge to strike the man. Violence is not his way and this man will not tempt him to blur his moral lines. One looks back at the dark haired woman and smiles. Having said that, he is looking forward to his new prototype meeting Thirty-Five. That should make for an interesting match.

10

Bray fills Garvan's glass with the last of Morgan's scotch. About ten minutes has gone past since he last spoke but Bray isn't pushing him. Whatever he's working through in his head, the memories are painful.

'If I tell you,' Garvan mumbles, startling Bray, 'it stays between you and me. No one can know about it.'

Bray nods his head. 'Of course.'

'Damn it. Okay. I grew up on the working class side of town. My parents worked as a housekeeper and gardener for one of the elite on the other side of the city. My folks worked damn hard and made sure I had everything I needed growing up. After school, I was allowed to go to the estate where my parents worked. The owners were a nice enough couple. Pompous, but tolerable. They had a son a few years older than me. We'd play together a bit but it was always on his terms. I wasn't allowed to touch any of his things in case I soiled them.' He snorts and takes a drink. 'It was the day before my fifteenth birthday when things went wrong. I got to the estate after school, just in time to see my parents being taken away by Foundation security. I was told they had been caught stealing from the owners.' He laughs. 'Stealing. It's bloody ridiculous. My parents were as honest as they came. There's no way they would have done that. Unfortunately, the elites were adamant and their word beat my parent's pleas. There wasn't even a trial. All the evidence was stacked against them. They were both sentenced to life in Tyrat and were shipped out on my birthday.'

Garvan pauses to take another drink and Bray joins him instead of sitting in awkward silence, unable to think of anything to say.

'I moved in with my aunt and carried on as best I could. I finished school and, as dictated by the Foundation, became an architect. I got married, had kids, did everything within the law and I was happy. A few years later I'm in Tyrat myself on another bogus charge. I'm an intelligent man but I couldn't figure out what the hell was going on. First my parents and now me—it didn't make sense... until he came to see me.'

'Who?'

Garvan takes a deep breath and his eyes burn with an anger Bray has never seen in him. 'One.'

'What?'

Garvan nods. 'Confused the hell out of me too. I was pulled out of my cosy cell and yanked into a room. One swept in like he was some sort of god. Guards bowing and scraping all around him. Everything made sense as soon as he took off the mask. It was Harvey, the elite's son.'

Bray shakes his head. 'I'm confused.'

'So was I. Irritating, spoilt Harvey became the illustrious One. He sat like a smug politician at the head of the table while I sat in my prison finest, chained to the table and floor opposite him. He then proceeded to brag about everything he'd done to mess up my life.

I still didn't get it. I'd done nothing to him. Why was he bothered with destroying me? But then he told me my parents overheard a conversation they weren't supposed to. To protect the content of the conversation, my parents were arrested on a bogus charge and carted away. He'd lost track of me. Thought the secret was safe until he found out I was on the colony design team. He didn't want to risk leaving me wandering around as a free man. He assumed my parents had told me the truth and that I'd ruin him sooner or later.'

'So you and your parents were arrested to protect

a secret?'

'Yeah. You see, little Harvey is adopted. My parents heard his parents talk about it and he thought they might have told me. They hadn't. The idiot told me himself in the prison. He's not the sharpest knife in the drawer.'

Bray holds up a hand. 'Stop there a minute. He's adopted. But he can't be, it's not allowed.'

Garvan smiles. 'Exactly. Only someone who is "pure bred" can take the position of One. His adoptive parents paid a lot of money to have his records altered. The only one who knows the truth is little old me, hence the bounty on my head.'

Bray leans back against the wall. 'But what about standard blood testing? That would have picked up he was adopted straight away.'

Garvan takes another mouthful of liquor before he answers. 'His adoptive parents had an endless supply of credits. They probably paid someone in the records department to hide the data. Who knows?' He shrugs. 'Who cares?'

Bray rubs his forehead. 'Just when I think I get the Foundation, something else crops up.'

Garvan nods. 'What I wouldn't give to squash that little toad under my boot. He must have thought he was home dry until I popped up on the security footage.' He smiles and takes another drink. 'Poor little Harvey must be sweating, worried I'm going to pull the rug out from under him.'

'Would you?'

Garvan snorts. 'Pull it out from under him? Damn it, I'd bury him in it.'

∞

One glides up the loading ramp of *Alpha*, his thick robe trailing along the ground behind him. He casts a critical eye over the personnel standing at attention in the cargo bay. A small smile touches his mouth. Nothing else he's experienced in his life gives him the same pleasure as the power of being One does. Even his presence in the room overrides every other order the personnel may have been given. Their lives stop until he has left, and that feeling is intoxicating. He follows Leeson to the back of the cargo hold and into a small storage room. His mask hides the grimace on his face. Forty-Three is lying on a gurney in the centre of the room with two Foundation crew. The cyborg's face is distorted by bruising, and blood stains his clothes from various injuries on his torso.

'Where was he found?'

Leeson gestures to the removed wall panel, showing the exposed cavity behind it. 'The body was hidden behind the wall. This room is not climate controlled. The smell was noticed by a crew member.'

'And the others?'

'In the same location. More disturbingly, they are both missing their left hand.'

One nods and examines the bodies. Forty-Three was severely beaten, while the other two had broken necks. Very different deaths. 'Where did the fight take place?'

Leeson frowns. 'Fight, sir?'

One rolls his eyes. 'Yes, Leeson. Clearly the cyborg was involved in a fight, or are you going to tell me he gave himself those injuries?'

Leeson shakes his head and examines the tablet in his hands. He scrolls through the data, still shaking his head. 'There's nothing in the report, sir.'

One clenches his fist to stop himself from striking the man. Instead he spins around and stalks back through the ship. He pauses in the cargo bay and inspects the cargo. He points to a badly stacked pile of crates in the far corner. 'Have those been touched since *Alpha* got back?'

The nearest crew member glances at the boxes then quickly shakes her head. 'No, sir.'

One weaves around the crates and crouches down in front of the upturned boxes. He runs a gloved finger along the smear of blood on the corner of one of the crates. He straightens and rubs his fingers together. 'As I said, Leeson, there was a fight. I want this area thoroughly examined. Every single speck of dirt tested. Do you understand?'

Leeson nods. 'Of course, sir.'

One steps off the ramp and into the air-conditioned bay. He takes a deep breath, thankful to be away from the stench. 'How long have they been dead?'

Leeson pauses and scratches his jaw. 'That is why I

contacted you. Testing shows they were killed... in this Sector.'

One turns his masked face towards Leeson. 'As I thought. Any more details?'

'I'm afraid Forty-Three was killed on board as the ship entered the Sector. The other two shortly after. Their killer is either a Foundation crew member—'

'Or they came to Earth from the Outer Sector,' One finishes. He stares at the giant form of *Alpha*, towering above them. She is his pride and joy. Just the thought that one of those Outer Sector rebels had the nerve to step foot on her sends his pulse racing. Without any identification or anywhere to hide, the damage they could cause would be minimal, but at this stage in proceedings, any damage was unwelcome.

'I want two teams examining every inch of the bodies. Leave nothing to chance. I want to know how and, more importantly, who killed them.'

'Of course.'

One turns his back on Leeson and marches through the bay to his private elevator. As he walks he contacts the rest of the Council, requesting that all data, all security from *Alpha*'s secret lab is carefully examined. He seriously doubts any intruder, no matter how efficient, would be able to breach her lower decks, but they are too close to take any chances. While he hopes someone from within the group killed the cyborg, he knows better. The prototype is still in the Outer Sector so it couldn't possibly have been him. The only conclusion is that another cyborg killed him, or Garvan is a bigger issue than he could ever have imagined.

Neither alternative sits very well with him.

11

Garvan joins Bray on the back porch, resting his arms on the wooden railing. He takes a deep breath and belches loudly. Bray raises an eyebrow and glances sideways at him.

'What?' Garvan asks. 'Blame the home cooking. It's going to be hard to go back to ship rations after all this delicious real food. Might have to live in the training room for a few weeks when I get back to *Perses*.'

Bray laughs. 'I know what you're saying. You know, if someone had told me a few weeks ago that you'd be comfortable in a situation like this I would have branded them a liar.'

Garvan cocks an eyebrow. 'Really? Why's that?'

Bray looks his friend up and down. 'You have to ask? You're built like a... well, a fighter I guess.'

Garvan smirks. 'Believe me, the old Wade Garvan wouldn't have known one end of a training room from the other.' He peers down at himself and his shoulders hunch. 'Doubt my own family would recognise me now.' He smiles and shrugs. 'Guess I'll have to be this Garvan a little longer. No point even thinking about seeing my family again until Harvey and the Foundation are out of the equation.' He straightens his shoulders and glances over at Bray. 'So, Commander, what about you? What's your plan for after we take the Foundation down, which we will do of course.'

There goes Bray's plan to keep the attention on Garvan. 'No plan really. *Perses* is my home now, that's all that matters. *Perses* is where it all began for me and, hopefully, where it will end too.'

'Retiring to Ultar or one of the other colonies not on the horizon?'

Bray snorts. 'I'd die of boredom.' He sounds convincing, but the intense look Garvan sends his way tells him he isn't fooled. In truth, before Gryffin came back on the scene he would have been more than happy to live out his days on Ultar with Terra. She had been the key element to his grand plan. With Gryffin's rising from the dead, he lost that plan when he lost Terra. Now, the idea of settling down anywhere leaves a bad taste in his mouth.

'Things aren't going to magically calm down once the Foundation is gone. The Hunters and Nomad have been trying to destroy each other for years. I know Sayber. As soon as the common enemy is gone, Gryffin will be in his sights again.'

'How's that going to work for you?'

Bray shrugs. 'I'm a Hunter. Always will be.'

'So, you'd stand by Sayber as he... well, kills your brother?'

'I'll stand by my Captain as he takes down our enemy.'

Garvan releases a long whistle. 'Interesting. You know, Commander, the more I hear about your family the more I realise how messed up you all are. The whole lot of you are perfect candidates for some serious therapy, you know that, right?'

Bray opens his mouth to argue, but his eyepiece chooses that moment to make its presence known. Bray rests his forehead on his clasped hands willing the searing pain to pick on someone else. Garvan places his hand on Bray's shoulder, quietly offering support. It takes a good five minutes before the pain recedes enough for him to raise his head again. He blinks a few times, clearing the tears from his eyes.

'You okay?'

Bray laughs, the sound resonating through his tender brain. 'Depends on your definition. We should get below before the drone does its pass.'

Without asking if he needs help, Garvan ducks under Bray's arm, supporting him as they stumble down the path to the barn. Once Bray is safely deposited on the couch, Garvan contacts the house to tell Morgan they've taken shelter for the night. Garvan lowers onto the table in front of the worn couch, his hands firmly clasped in front of him. 'It's getting worse.'

Even though it's a statement rather than a question, Bray nods slowly. 'Think the Scientist's design needs a bit of work.'

Garvan forces a small smile on his face. 'You want me to get you anything?'

'I'll be fine in a minute. Hey, don't look so worried. You have to admit I'm keeping things interesting for you.'

Garvan snorts. 'You do that. Prison was a relaxing holiday compared to all this mess.' Garvan quiets for a moment then asks the question Bray was hoping to dodge for a bit longer, 'When are you going to tell your family about Gryffin?'

Bray glares at Garvan as he swivels into a sitting position on the couch. 'I will tell them. I just don't know how or when.'

Garvan makes a face and shakes his head. 'Nice try, Bray, but I'm not buying it. You and I both know you're stalling. Just get them together and tell them.'

'Yeah, right,' Bray replies sarcastically. 'C'mon, Garvan, how exactly am I supposed to even begin that conversation?' Bray rubs his forehead and squeezes his eyes shut. 'I don't know what to say. I can't just jump in with "By the way, Daegan's still alive."'

'Daegan's alive?' Bray and Garvan glance at each other before slowly peeking over their shoulders at Morgan.

Garvan meets Bray's eyes and grimaces. 'Think that problem just sorted itself out,' Garvan mumbles. He smiles apologetically at Bray, pats him on the back then makes a swift get-away into one of the bedrooms.

'Did I hear you right? Is Daegan alive?' Morgan asks again.

Bray's first instinct is to lie. Knowing the truth about both Daegan and himself will only hurt them. Erin climbs down the steps and stops beside her father, a plate of cake in each hand. She pauses and glances between Bray and her father. 'What are you two arguing about now?'

Morgan takes a step closer to Bray, not letting the younger man out of his gaze. 'Answer my question. Is Daegan still alive?'

Erin places the plates on the step behind her. 'Daegan's alive? What are you talking about?'

The lie is planned and primed, ready to go, but something happens at the last minute. Bray's brain and mouth have a fatal breakdown in communication. 'Yes. Daegan's alive.'

Morgan lowers to the step behind him and focuses on Bray. 'You need to talk. We need to know everything.'

Bray waits a few seconds, but a hole doesn't appear in front of him to disappear into. What he wouldn't give for a speedy dodge from this conversation. Instead of saying anything, he nods once. Without waiting for an invitation, Erin and Morgan take a seat to either side of him.

'Bray.' He peers up at Morgan. 'Tell us what you know.'

'It's a complicated mess and I don't know if you really want to hear it.'

'But he's alive, right?' Morgan asks.

'Well, yes, but it's not that simple. He's not... he doesn't...' Bray blows out a breath, struggling to find the right words.

Morgan squeezes Bray's arm. 'Hey, whatever it is, we'll deal with it.

∞

Bray spends the next hour filling Morgan and Erin in on the last few years. He explains how he was arrested for smuggling guns and ended up in Tyrat. How Avoca broke him out and how they worked together to repair the horror left by the Foundation's cyborg program.

His voice falters slightly as he describes what happened to him on the freighter with the Scientist and how he spent the next few weeks in a coma. He skips over his relationship with Terra and how he had returned to *Perses* in shame, regretting having given her so much of his heart.

When he details their attack on the prisons and

freeing Garvan, the story sounds surreal, even to him. Once he has finished his massively edited version of the events, he stares down at his boots, not wanting to see the disappointment on their faces. He hasn't exactly done anything to make them proud since he left twelve years ago.

'That's one hell of a story, son.'

Bray lifts his head and frowns. Instead of disappointment, he can only see concern on Morgan's face.

Erin leans forward, wrapping her arms around her torso. 'Have to admit, I now know why the Foundation were—sorry are, so concerned about Gryffin and your group of rebels.'

'So,' Morgan continues, 'where does Daegan come in to all this? You haven't mentioned him once.'

Bray runs a hand through his hair. 'Well, I've actually been talking about him for a while. Gryffin is Daegan.'

After an incredibly awkward silence Morgan is the first to voice his shock. 'I don't understand? How is that possible? He disappeared. How can he be this... Gryffin person? It doesn't make any sense.'

'I still don't know all the details, but the Foundation took Daegan when he was a child. He was brought to a facility where he was experimented on and modified.' Bray rubs the metal beside his eye.

'The same thing that happened to you?' Erin asks, quietly.

Bray shakes his head. 'Gryffin's mods are far more

extensive. I was lucky that Sayber got me out before I had too much work done. I'm just stuck with the piece at my eye and a plate on my chest.'

'And Daegan?' Morgan asks. 'Is he a machine?

'He's not a machine. He's human.' Bray smiles. 'In fact, apart from the visible metal he looks like an older Daegan. It's only on the surface though. Unlike me, he's had a lot of work internally. His organs are all supported by implants, there's a large control implant on his brain, the bottom half of his right arm is metal as is his right thigh. He's also got a robotic left eye and some plating on his chest.'

'My God,' Morgan mutters. 'How long did they have him?'

'About five years. The Nomad found him, brought him back from near death and he worked his way up the ranks. He's the Captain, well, the High Commander actually. He's done pretty good for himself.'

Morgan stands and shuffles to the counter in the kitchenette. He leans on the surface, gripping the edge tightly, the muscles in his arm clenching as he pushes against it. Morgan suddenly shouts and kicks the cupboard at his feet over and over. The wood surrenders to the blows, splintering into pieces. Erin places her hand on her father's back but he slides out of her reach.

'No, Erin!' He storms up the stairs, slamming the trap door shut after him.

Erin slumps down on the bottom step, a far-away

look on her face. Bray lowers beside her, but doesn't touch her. 'You okay?'

She laughs harshly and wipes under her eyes. 'Okay? No I'm not okay. I'm far from okay. You and Daegan are more than cousins to me. You know that.' She wipes her eyes again and hugs her arms tight to her chest. 'You were tortured, Bray. You both were.' She faces him and reaches out with a trembling hand to touch his implant. 'That's... in you?'

Bray nods. 'All the implants are.' He shrugs and tries to put a convincing smile on his face. 'It's not that—'

'Don't you dare say it's not that bad. I'm not an idiot, Bray. Having metal in and on your body is pretty bad. Having it on there by force is even worse.' She sniffs and gets up, her arms wrapped tightly around her torso. 'I can't believe I'm going to say this, but does that make you and Daegan cyborgs?'

Bray shrugs. 'I guess that's the best way to describe it. Not too keen on the term though.'

Erin thrusts both hands through her hair as she stares up at the ceiling. 'I can't get my head around this. I should go after Dad.'

'I'll go,' Bray offers. 'You stay here, okay?'

She nods weakly and slumps onto the couch. Bray focuses on his distraught cousin but doesn't know how to make things better for her. Hell, he doesn't know how to deal with the mess himself. What good could he be to anyone else?

He checks that the sky is clear of drones before

running up the path to the house. He checks the ground floor of the house quickly, stopping his search when he notices the cupboard housing the scotch is empty. He curses under his breath and shuts the back door behind him. He stands on the back porch and scans the yard, finally spotting his uncle leaning against the railings by the lake.

Bray joins him and watches the glowing city lights in the distance. 'How much have you had?' he asks, nodding at the bottle in Morgan's hand.

His uncle snorts and shakes his head. 'More than my quota, that's for sure.'

'Is it helping?'

'Doubt anything could.' Morgan takes another swig, grimacing as he lowers the bottle. 'This Scientist that hurt you both,' Morgan snarls. 'That bastard have a name?'

'Morgan—'

'Name, Bray,' he growls.

'Callum Rush.'

Morgan's brows leap up. 'That's the same name as Jensen's best friend. It couldn't be him... could it?'

'You know Jensen?' Bray asks in surprise.

Morgan frowns at Bray. 'You know Jensen?'

'Well, yeah. He's the Captain of the Foundation ship, Infinity. The ship was sent to the Outer Sector to prep for colonisation. After learning about everything the Foundation did, Roman stole the ship and is now working with the Outer Sector colonists.'

Morgan nods approvingly and some of the tension

seems to drain from his shoulders. 'Has he met Daegan—I mean Gryffin? Damn it, these names are going to confuse the hell out of me.'

Bray narrows his eyes. 'You know about Roman and Daegan, don't you?'

Morgan nods slowly and slides down to sit on the ground. He takes another swig, wiping his mouth on his sleeve. He stares up at the night sky, a small smile on his face.

'Maggie and I were damn close. Of course I knew who Daegan's father was. When she got pregnant, it wasn't hard to figure it out.' He blows out a breath. 'For months Maggie and Jensen were inseparable, and I mean inseparable. They went everywhere together. Mum and Dad thought she was far too young to be so serious, but they didn't interfere. Jensen was from a very good family. Looking at it from a Foundation viewpoint, he was a hell of a good prospect. There was a lot of suitors interested in him, but he only had eyes for Maggie.'

'What happened?' Bray asks, curiosity getting a firm grip on him.

'Well, as I said, our parents had no objection. Jensen was a decent fellow and he worshipped the ground Maggie walked on. The problem was his folks. They tried to get him to marry one of the more suitable prospects but he put his foot down. Unable to convince him otherwise, they pulled a dirty trick from their bag. They enlisted him in the fleet. It was something he couldn't object to or argue against. A few weeks later, he was gone.'

Bray takes a few breaths to steady the sinking feeling in his stomach. While he loved his own father, he can't help but be upset by what happened to his mother and Jensen. 'When did she find out she was pregnant?'

'A few weeks after he left. His parents refused to see her so she tried other ways of contacting him. Seems they had shut down all avenues of communication. I tried to help her, but...' Morgan shrugs. 'She had no choice but to give up. So, how did Jensen find out about Daegan?'

'One of his crew shot Gryffin. They tested the blood on the round and found a match to Roman.'

Morgan shakes his head. 'I can't believe he knows. Maggie wanted to tell him for so long. So, do they get along with each other?'

Bray makes a face. 'Gryffin isn't the easiest to have a relationship with. Roman wants more, but... well, let's just say Gryffin isn't too keen on the idea. I think Roman is happy enough even knowing about him.'

Morgan sighs loudly and takes another drink. 'I never imagined Daegan... I mean I always hoped he was alive. Out there somewhere in the big wide galaxy living it up.' He makes a face and kicks at the ground by his feet. 'Being experimented on didn't enter my mind. Damn it.' He raises the bottle to his mouth but Erin appears out of the night and pulls it away before he can drink.

She crouches down in front of her father. 'That

won't help, Dad.'

'How can the Foundation do something like this?'

She shakes her head. 'I don't know.' She sits opposite him, her legs tucked under her. 'I didn't know anything,' Erin's mumbled statement is barely audible.

'Didn't know what?' Bray asks.

'I didn't know what the Foundation was doing... is doing. There could be people in the HQ right now being tortured like you and Daegan were. How could I not know that?'

'The Foundation have been hiding it for decades, Erin,' Bray says. 'There's no way they would have done anything to make people suspicious. They were kidnapping children. If people knew that, the Foundation would be under a bit of pressure to explain themselves.'

Erin curses and shakes her head. 'I'm sorry, Bray.'

Bray is confused by the sudden apology. 'What the hell for?'

'For being sucked in like some damn rookie. I've been protecting these people. Damn it, I've fought for them.'

Morgan rests his hand on her shoulder. 'Blaming yourself is ridiculous. The Foundation are the ones that have a hell of a lot to answer for.'

'Daegan was ten, Dad.'

Morgan nods slowly. 'I know.'

'Guys, he's alive,' Bray says. 'And there's a lot of people in the Outer Sector itching to make the

Foundation pay.'

'Yeah he's alive,' Morgan says. 'But at what expense?'

'He's doing fine,' Bray lies. They've had a big enough shock without learning that last time he saw his brother, he was in bad shape with half his metal leg sticking out through his flesh.

'And you?' Erin asks.

Bray hopes his smile is convincing. 'I'm fine too. Well, apart from the issues my eyepiece is giving me lately. The cyborg on *Alpha* gave me a fairly good thump. Might have done some damage.'

'Can you not take the metal parts off?' Morgan asks.

'Believe me, I'd like nothing more. Problem is, everything we know about the implants we've picked up along the way. The only ones with the answers Gryffin and I need are in the Council HQ.'

'So, that's why you were on *Alpha*?'

Bray nods at Erin. 'The Scientist's system was taken from the colony. That information can't be left in the Foundation's hands. If they create more like Gryffin we're all in serious trouble.'

12

Bray picks up a stone and hurls it across the lake. The loud splash disturbs the otherwise quiet morning. He volleys another stone into the water and paces the shore, scattering pebbles as he kicks at the ground. Bray runs a hand through his hair, wincing as he brushes against the sensitive implant on the side of his head. The pain from the damn thing is only getting worse. His left eye twitches uncontrollably as the pain burrows into the side of his face. He shouts and slams his fist against a tree.

'Bit of an unfair scrap, Bray. You got a problem with trees?'

He spins quickly and faces Erin. 'You're back.'

She leans against a large tree by the water's edge and tucks her hair behind her ear. 'It appears so. What's got you in such a mood?'

'I'm not good at sitting around doing nothing.'

She nods and smiles. 'In other words, you weren't happy about letting me take the lead today. I hate to break it to you, but you didn't really have much of a choice. I have to go to work.'

'Yeah but I should have—'

'Should have what? Held my hand while I did my days' work? C'mon, Bray. I'm a big girl now and I'm head of security. I think I can manage to do my job without you holding my hand.'

'I know. Ignore me. I'm going crazy being stuck on the ground for so long,' he says while lowering to the ground. 'How was work? Did you discover anything useful?'

She sits opposite him, tucking her legs under her. 'Yes and no.'

'Very helpful, care to elaborate?'

'Well, *Alpha* is still on the surface and, at the moment, she'll be staying there. I was able to do a quick recon and couldn't find anything. She's empty. There is a lot of cargo waiting to be loaded but nothing matching the crates you described.'

'Cargo? Like what?'

Erin shrugs. 'Medical supplies mainly, you know like theatre packs, anaesthetic, drugs, stuff like that. There was a box of electronic components. I think it was scrap.'

Bray peers at a spot on the grass as the realisation suddenly hits him. 'Where's she going?'

'Nowhere. According to the flight schedule for the next week, she's staying put.'

Bray glances back to Erin. 'It's on *Alpha*.'

She frowns and wrinkles her nose. 'What is?'

'The new cyborg lab.'

Erin opens her mouth to question him, but shuts it again as she figures it all out. 'The supplies, the components... it's not scrap.'

Bray taps his facial implant. 'Depends on your definition.'

Erin leans back against the tree and draws her knees up to her chest. 'Of course. It makes perfect sense. With the lab on *Alpha*, it's portable. All they have to do is relocate the ship and the lab stays intact and fully operational. Damn it. That gives us a pretty big problem. Like I said before, *Alpha* is solely for Council use. Apart from her main engineering deck and the cargo hold, everything else is locked down. It's all top secret.'

'Great,' Bray mutters, taking his frustration out on an unsuspecting pebble by hurtling into the lake. 'So, we're back at square one.'

Erin smirks. 'I didn't say that.' She jumps to her feet and offer her hand to help Bray up. 'I think I might just be a damn genius.'

Without a word, Bray hurries after Erin into the house. She races to the small room at the back of the house serving as an office and sits down at Morgan's unit.

'What are you doing?'

She grins widely at Bray as she boots the system up. The grin stays on her face as she punches in a twenty-digit code to secure the system, then enters another longer code to access her Foundation system.

'I may have something else that could help us out. I just need to make sure no one followed my orders yet.' She frowns at the screen as it shifts to an aerial view of the cargo hold. *Alpha*'s hulking form dwarfs everything to the right of the screen.

'Bloody hell, Erin. That's great.'

She cocks her head to the side. 'Yes and no. I can't stay in the system too long. Don't want to attract attention. Anyway, a few days ago I ordered a new batch of surveillance drones. Before I left today, I ordered that they be packed away.' She zooms in, carefully examining every crate in the bay. 'Ah ha!' she exclaims. 'I've never been happier to have been ignored.' She taps the screen zooming in on the box even more. 'That's it.'

Bray frowns. 'And what's so great about that?'

She tuts and shakes her head. 'Oh ye of little faith.' She turns back to the screen and pulls up a side control panel. The lights on one of the palm sized drones flashes as it rises out of the crate.

Bray drops into the chair beside her. 'Okay, now I'm impressed.'

'I am a woman of many talents. Now shut up while I concentrate.' She chews her bottom lip as she guides the small craft out of the box and behind another crate. It quickly flies up the ramp and disappears into the ship. Erin taps the screen and the view switches to the camera on the drone. Bray opens his mouth to speak but she holds up a finger to silence him again. The drone weaves under the crates by the door before moving to the large stack towards the back of the bay. Erin zooms out and nods towards the plastic side of the crate. 'Those are the components.'

Bray's eyes narrow as he recognises part of the metal work. 'Yep, they're implants. Damn it. Seems like they're about to start.'

'If they haven't already.' She guides the small robot away from the cargo hold and into a large air vent at the entrance to the adjoining corridor. 'Up or down?'

'Up or down what?'

'The lab.'

Bray studies the desk in front of him then focuses on the screen again. 'Down.'

'Sure?'

He nods. 'We've come across two of them so far. One was on the lower decks and the other was underground.' He shrugs. 'Best I can offer.'

She looks back at the drone. 'I'll go for that then.' She directs the drone along the vent and down the first path she can take. As the drone drops through the ship, she displays another screen and brings up a schematic.

'What's that?'

'*Alpha*.'

'Hang on, you have schematics?'

'Of course I don't. Our little friend is mapping it for us.'

Bray focuses back on the screen and realises she's right. The further the drone travels into *Alpha*, the larger the branches of the schematic grow. 'How deep can you go?'

She shrugs. 'Depends on how deep we're allowed to. If you are right and the lab is on board, I imagine we'll hit against some kind of defence as we get closer. The Council aren't just going to let anyone or anything wander around in there.' She curses and stops the drone in its path. 'And here we are.'

'The lab?'

'Defences.' She points to the flashing line of code on the bottom of the screen. 'We go any further and they'll know we've been here. We should probably head back before we push our luck.'

Bray silently examines the map as Erin guides the drone back to its friends in the crate. The lab has to be on board—he just knows it.

Erin shuts the robot down, making sure to overload its memory banks before she comes out of the system.

'Won't that attract attention?'

'Out of a delivery of a thousand we always have a few failures.' She spins the chair around and crosses her legs. 'So, what's the great plan?'

'Honestly? I haven't got a clue. Just a shame we

can't sneak around like the drone.'

'Come on, Bray. The plan is easy. It's the details we have to iron out.'

He leans back and crosses his arms. 'Is that right. Okay, let's hear it.'

'We break into *Alpha*, copy the info, destroy the units and get you back to the Outer Sector.'

Bray's mouth opens and closes a few times until he finally links his brain. 'Hang on, we?'

She leans forward and meets Bray's eyes. 'You said it yourself. The Foundation can't have this information. So, let's go get it.'

∞

Morgan's hearty laugh echoes in the still house. Bray bites back a curse and silently waits while his uncle gets himself together. He glances at Erin. His cousin shrugs, not offering any advice. Garvan on the other hand just silently stares at him, which doesn't fill Bray with much confidence. Morgan wipes his eyes and takes a deep breath.

'Cheers, Bray. I needed that.'

'I'm serious.'

Morgan nods. 'So am I. I haven't laughed like that for a long time.'

Bray clenches his jaw and takes a few seconds to get himself together. He knows his plan to go back to the Foundation HQ, and board *Alpha* is a risky one, but Morgan could at least have the decency to listen to all the details before he laughs the whole thing off as a big joke.

'You finished yet?'

Morgan nods. 'For now. Unless of course you have something else stupid to say.'

'It's not stupid. The Foundation are planning something. We can all agree on that, right?'

Morgan scratches his eyebrow. 'That still doesn't mean there's anything we can do about it. What's your plan—knock on the door, ask if we can have a peek around for their secret cyborg information and then stroll out with the unit tucked under your arm? It's too risky.'

Bray is about to argue his point when Erin clears her throat and speaks, 'That's where I come in. *Alpha* is linked to the base at a number of points. According to the scan I did of the cargo hold, the elevator the Council uses to access her should be to the north side of the compound. With a bit of manoeuvring, we should be able to get to her without stepping foot in the base. '

Morgan shakes his head. 'No way. If you're caught, your career is over. Hell, they'll sentence you to death.'

'Career? What career. All I've been doing is protecting a lie. We spent years searching for Daegan with the Foundation's help. They put on this elaborate charade, said they were doing everything they could to locate him while they were the ones that had him the whole time. I'm done living a lie, Dad.'

'So, what are you saying?' Morgan asks. 'You're just going to throw away your career and everything you've worked so hard for?'

'No, Dad. I'm saying that I want to use my skills and my position, to stop a corrupt group from hurting innocent people. It's what I signed up to do. I just never thought that the group I'd be fighting would be the Foundation.'

Morgan gets to his feet and paces in front of them. 'This is bloody ridiculous. If you're caught you'll all be killed or sealed in Tyrat for the rest of your short lives. You know that, right?'

Erin props her feet up on the chair opposite her. 'Have a little faith, Dad. I know HQ like the back of my hand. I can lead us safely through the building to *Alpha.*'

'Then what? She's the Council's ship, Erin. They're not going to let you have a wander around. It's too much of a risk. You can't go.'

'I'm not asking for your permission, Dad,' Erin replies. 'Those two clowns don't have a hope without me and you know it. They can pretend to be as macho as they want but they need my help.'

Bray looks across at Garvan, but only gets a shrug in reply. 'I guess we don't have a choice.'

Morgan grunts and leans back in his chair, understandably unhappy about Erin's offer of help. 'Okay, I'll play along with this nonsense for a minute. So, you're in the building and manage to get on to *Alpha.* What then? Any information they have is going to be well and truly secured. And you don't even know where it's stored.'

'I would imagine it's in the bowels of the ship,' Erin says. 'The bottom decks are locked down for private use by the Council. If One has brought the project back to Earth, it makes sense it would be located there.'

'Wouldn't he want it as far from the HQ as possible?' Morgan asks. 'Isn't it risky having it in the middle of a highly populated area, especially on a ship?'

'One is a control freak,' Garvan says. Everyone turns to look at him, surprised by the information.

'You know him?' Erin asks.

Garvan nods. 'In a different lifetime. If this is his baby, there's no way he'll let anyone else look after it. He'll have the work nearby so he can check in regularly. If he's making any more cyborgs, *Alpha* is a good choice.'

Erin leans forward and makes a face. 'Hang on, are you saying there could be more Gryffin-like cyborgs waiting to greet us?'

'No,' Bray says, and Erin visibly relaxes. 'They'll probably be... for want of a better description... better made than Gryffin.'

'That's good to know.' Garvan snatches his drink and empties the glass.

Morgan nods at Garvan. 'Couldn't have said it better myself. Damn it, Bray. From what you've said, it sounds like what they did to Gryffin means he could take all of you down without any effort. What's your plan if you meet anything more advanced than him?'

'That's why we have to go, and soon. We need to see what they're up to, and copy or destroy the data before they create an unstoppable army,' Bray says.

'What about Gryffin?'

Bray turns to Erin and her blue eyes immediately lock on to him. 'What about him?'

'You're all worried about the possible existence of new cyborgs. Excuse the phrasing, but the original one is on your side. Why not bring him in?'

It's a thought that's entered Bray's mind more than once, but it's not going to happen. 'I'd give anything to have him fighting with us, believe me. By the time we figure out a way to contact Ultar and get him here, it could be too late.' He doesn't bother muddying the waters with talk of his implant issues. 'No, we're going to have to figure this out on our own.'

Morgan refills his glass with scotch, not caring about the imposed drinking limit. 'Okay geniuses, I have another one for you. What about Garvan? They have his face on the wanted list. As soon as they see him, he'll be captured.'

'Exactly,' Erin replies. 'And that's what we want.'

'We do?' Garvan replies. 'Something I said, Commander?'

She squeezes his arm. 'Believe me, getting you captured is the last thing I want, but it could work in our favour. We still need some way of getting in to the lab. You have a Foundation transmitter?'

Garvan nods slowly. 'They deactivated it when I got to Tyrat.'

Erin leans forward, her expression lightening as she rapidly speaks. 'I can reactivate it. As soon as you're taken down to the facility, we can track it.'

'What makes you think Garvan will be taken anywhere near there?' Bray asks.

'All prisoners we've apprehended lately are taken to *Alpha*. I've been told they're being taken off-world for rehabilitation.' Her eyes focus on the ground, and the excitement that was present a moment before, ebbs away. 'Yeah, well, we all know that's not true. I strongly believe they're being taken to the lab. It's the only explanation. They're certainly not leaving the facility.'

Morgan takes another mouthful before he speaks again. 'Sounds like a lot of assumptions.'

Erin shrugs. 'It's the best I can do. Once we're in, I can try to access systems, but if I do it now, it'll only flag to my superiors. The last thing I want to do now is attract any attention to what we're planning.'

'Which revolves around handing me over to the Foundation,' Garvan replies. 'Would have been nice if someone gave me the heads up.' He gets to his feet and frowns down at Bray. 'Fellow Hunter, huh. Sure doesn't feel like that.' He turns around and walks away without another word.

Bray takes a deep breath and knocks on Garvan's bedroom door. The way his friend left the meeting worried him. Bray may not have known him for long, but he knows him well enough to see Garvan has a serious issue with their plan. His silence during the meeting was a dead giveaway.

Garvan pulls the door open and quietly peers down at Bray.

'We need to talk.'

Garvan crosses his arms defensively. 'Is that so? Seems I'm nothing but a pawn in your plan. What's to talk about?'

Bray nudges past the larger man and lowers on to

the bed. Garvan glares at him over his shoulder before he shuts the door and leans against the wall.

'I'm not asking you to do this. Erin knows what she's talking about when it comes to HQ and the Council, but I'm not willing to put your life on the line. I don't want you to do this so there's no problem. We'll think of something else.'

Garvan's eyes narrow as he strides across the room and sits on the chair by the far wall. 'What you're planning, leaving aside my part, it's a one-way trip, Commander. You and I both know it. As soon as they get a whiff of your Hunter ass, you'll be back in prison, if you're lucky. They might just decide to string you up as a trophy beside your cousin. Hang you from the main square so the dutiful people can see how great their government is at catching the bad guys. You should leave Earth while you still can... we all should.'

'I can't go yet.'

Garvan rubs his chin. 'Yes, you can. You do realise we're not on a city break, right? We're a Hunter and an escaped convict on Earth. I think that rules out extending our vacation.'

'I came here to get the files on the project. I can't leave while the Foundation still have access to the information.'

'You can if I hit you on the head and haul you back.'

'I'm being serious, Garvan.'

'So am I, Commander. Your family took one hell of

a risk hiding us. They don't need a death sentence as a thank you. Your hair-brained idea include their safety at all?'

'Of course it does. Leaving that information with the Foundation doesn't ensure anyone's safety. In a couple of months, there could be an army of Gryffin's ready and more than able to take over the Outer Sector. The Hunters and Nomad could be wiped out before we can even formulate a defence.'

'Your family could be wiped out if we stay here any longer.' Garvan runs a hand over his hair. 'Listen, Bray, I've got your back, you know I do, but this... it's a bit too crazy, even for me.'

'I can't leave Earth until I get that information. We're so close. There won't be another opportunity like this. We'd be crazy to turn it down.'

Garvan snorts. 'Crazy is right, but I'm using that to describe you and this plan.' Garvan rests his head against the wooden wall panel. 'Okay, let's suspend reason for a moment. How exactly do you know they haven't already used the information? What if there is an army of the damn things lying in wait for us? What then?' He gestures to Bray. 'Go on. I'm all ears.'

Bray opens his mouth, then shuts it again and makes a face.

'Exactly as I thought.'

'I need to do this, Garvan.'

Garvan shakes his head and curses loudly. 'What's the real reason?'

'I've told you.'

'I may have spent the last few years talking to cockroaches, but I'm not an idiot. Be honest with me.'

'Fine. It's my eye, okay.'

'Now I'm even more confused. Your eye is making you do stupid things?'

Bray rolls his eyes at Garvan. 'That's not what I mean.' He taps the side of his face next to his left eye. 'This is... I don't know how to explain it... it's changing.'

Garvan frowns. 'I'm still in the confused camp.'

'Apart from the bursts of pain which are getting worse, my eye is also... changing colour.'

Garvan leans down to examine Bray's eye. 'Damn. So it is. When did that start?'

Bray shrugs. 'I noticed it just after we got here. I don't know if the blow from Forty-Three had anything to do with it or not. I just get the feeling something is going on with it. With me.'

Garvan nods slowly. 'I hear you. Do you think there's something on the Foundation system that can explain what's happening?'

'Partly, I guess. What if they've... modified me, like they did with Gryffin.'

Garvan shudders. 'Not a happy image.'

'Exactly.' Bray shrugs. 'I need to get the information to know for sure. It could help Gryffin too. And you can wipe that smug smile off your face before I remove it for you.'

Garvan holds up his hands in surrender. 'Just interesting to hear you speaking like that about him.'

Bray sighs loudly. 'It's impossible not to think about Mum and Dad right now. They wouldn't want me to hate him. What happened... it's not his fault. I just need to get my head to accept that. I know one thing for sure—my folks would kick my ass if they knew I was even thinking of turning my back on Gryffin. I can't change what happened to them, to him, or to me, but I can try to do something about our future.'

'Goddammit.' Garvan makes a face. 'Fine. I'll do it.'

'I'm not asking you to.'

'I know. I still owe you. I can't be your hero if I'm not even in the same place as you. Besides,' Garvan holds his hand against his heart, 'that speech got me just here, Commander.'

'Now who's being a jackass.'

Garvan drops his arm to his side. 'What? I was deeply moved, Commander.'

'Idiot.' Bray shakes his head and walks away, ignoring the large grin on his friend's face.

∞

'Can I talk to you for a minute?'

Garvan glances up from his book, smiling when he sees Erin standing at the top of the stairs leading down to the underground apartment. 'Of course.'

'Where's Bray?'

'Working on the transport with your dad. I think

it's their uncle and nephew bonding time so I'm staying well clear.'

'Is he okay?'

Garvan smiles. 'Of course.'

She sits beside him, brushing her hair behind her ear. 'I didn't get the rank of Commander by not seeing what's going on around me.' She makes a face and stares at Bray's bedroom door. 'Well, apart from what the Foundation were up to of course. What I mean is that I know something's up with his modifications. Bray was in his fair share of scraps when he was a child. He would have fought his own shadow some days given the chance. I saw Mum patch him up enough times over the years to know when he's in pain and hiding it.'

Garvan puts his book on the table and turns to face Erin. 'He'll be just fine. I promise.'

She nods and smiles widely. 'Understood. Male pride and covering for your ship mate. Seems the rules are the same wherever you are.'

He grins but doesn't confirm or deny her statement. 'So, is that what you wanted to ask me?'

'No. Actually, I wanted to see if things are okay... if we're okay after my offering to have you arrested without asking you first.'

Garvan laughs and rests his arm on the back of the chair. 'I've never been offered up as bait so fast before. It just took me by surprise. It's all good.'

Erin blushes slightly. Usually she seems so confident and sure of herself. Blushing isn't something he thought she would ever do. 'That's good. I think this whole thing with my cousins has affected my judgement a little.'

'It's understandable. They were both dead. It's a lot to take in.'

'That's an understatement.' She glances away from him. 'You know, my whole life has been working towards my assigned rank in the Foundation. For as long as I can remember, I knew I would have a position in the HQ. When I surpassed my designated role, I was over the moon. It was a hell of an achievement.'

'You don't have to tell me that. You should be proud.'

She looks at him again, her blue eyes sparkling. If he didn't know better he'd say she was about to cry. 'I was until I learnt the truth. Being a part of the Foundation is not something to be proud of anymore—not after what they've done.' She shuffles nearer to him. 'What I'm trying to say, and this is between you and me, is that I envy Bray the life he's had. I always thought he was a fool rebelling against the Foundation way. Why wouldn't he want to be the best he could be? But I've realised, after hearing the truth, that I wish I had taken the chance he did.'

Garvan rests his head on his hand and frowns. 'You don't mean that.'

She nods with conviction. 'I do. He's lived. Really lived. I know the modifications are horrible and my heart bleeds for both of them, but he's seen a lot more of the universe than I have.'

'Yeah, but it's not all been sweetness and light.' He scratches the stubble on his cheek as he thinks about what to say next. 'I don't know much about what happened to Bray when he left here, but I do know, like most people in the Outer Sector, things weren't easy for him. There's more to life than just seeing the sights. There's the simple things like having somewhere to lay your head, being around people who give a damn about you. I know a lot of people who would trade their whole lives for one day like that.'

'Seriously?'

He nods. 'I'll let you in on a little secret. Tyrat taught me a harsh lesson. Enjoy what you have. There's no point regretting or wishing we did things differently. There's nothing we can do about it. The only thing we can do is make the right decision based on where we are in our life at this moment.'

'Sounds like a good philosophy. Does it work?'

Garvan makes a face. 'Sometimes. The most important thing is that you know the truth and you want to do something about it. Not a lot of people would put their career, their lives, on the line to do the right thing. You should be proud of that.'

She smiles at him. 'Thanks. So, what about you? How did you get tangled up in all this?'

Garvan releases a long breath and focuses on a spot on the floor. 'Long story.'

'Do you have family on Earth?'

He shakes his head. 'My wife, son, and daughter are on Mars as far as I know.'

She glances down at his hand. 'You don't wear a ring. I just assumed...'

Garvan reaches under his shirt and pulls out a chain with a platinum ring threaded on it. 'I got used to hiding it on Tyrat.' He looks down at the ring turning slowly on its chain. 'I haven't seen her or my kids since I was arrested.' He slips the ring back under his top and smiles. 'I don't even know if they are on Mars, not for sure at least.'

'Do you want me to do a search for them? On the system I mean.'

Garvan pauses for a moment, tempted to jump at her offer. 'Nah. Thanks anyway, but I'm not sure I'm ready for that. My head needs to be focused on what's going on here. If I let myself think about them, if I know what they've achieved without me...' He smiles sadly and looks back at her. 'I have to leave them locked in here for the moment.' He taps a finger against his chest, directly over his heart. 'At least I know they're safe in here.'

Anything else Garvan was going to say is cut off when Erin leans over and kisses him. Frozen in shock, he doesn't fight her for the first few seconds, then his brain reboots. He gently nudges her away, shaking his head. 'I'm sorry, Erin. I can't do this.'

Erin leaps to her feet, colour racing up her face. 'I'm so, so sorry, Garvan. I don't know what came over me.'

He gets up and steps towards her but she backs away. 'Hey, it's more than okay, Erin. Really. I'm flattered. It's been a hell of a long time since anyone showed interest in me like that, but—'

'You don't have to explain.' She turns away, pulling her hair back from her face with both hands. 'As I said, my judgement is affected.' She laughs awkwardly and looks at him again. 'You must think I'm terrible. Here you are, talking about your wife and family, and I take that as an invitation to kiss you. I'm truly sorry, Garvan. Can we please forget this ever happened?'

Garvan forces a smile. 'Of course. Already done.'

Erin nods briskly then races up the stairs. Garvan slumps back on to the couch and runs a hand over his lips.

'Where the hell did that come from?' He lies back and stares up at the ceiling. He never thought about being with anyone other than his wife—ever. But when Erin kissed him... He sighs deeply. He lost all contact with his family the day One had him locked up. He doesn't even know if they're alive. For all he knows, his wife is happily remarried and has moved on from him. He shakes his head. That may be the case but he made a promise to her when they got married. While their marriage was one of convenience rather than love, it's still a marriage.

He gets up and grabs a glass of water before lying on his bed. An hour later he's still staring at the ceiling, his thoughts focused more on Erin than his wife.

14

'It's time.'

Bray nods at Garvan, hating that it's come to this. His decision to go to Foundation HQ is the right one. He's positive of that. The thing he didn't factor in is how it will affect his family. By Erin and Morgan insisting on tagging along, they've transformed their future on Earth drastically. The Foundation isn't stupid. It won't take them long to figure out how they broke in to HQ. They'll trace it back to Erin, then Morgan.

If they're to survive beyond today, they'll need to leave their life on the surface behind. Bray would never make the suggestion himself. He hoped that

Erin would address the subject with her father and they'd make the decision without him. Erin had taken her father aside last night, and in less than half an hour they were packing up everything they needed to continue a life elsewhere.

Morgan had transferred ownership of the house and any remaining livestock to their nearest neighbour a few miles away. The transfer wouldn't take effect until they were far away from Earth so it wouldn't arouse suspicion.

Bray's surprised at how accepting Morgan and Erin are of their changing circumstances. A few days ago, he would have never thought they would turn against the Foundation, never mind leave Earth to live an uncertain life... well, who knows where. There's no way Bray's little transport can make the journey to the Outer Sector. A lot is depending on his exit plan, which at the moment, is less than guaranteed.

Morgan leaves to do a final check of all the rooms again. Erin picks her bag off the ground and shuffles around Garvan, both blushing slightly as they repeatedly bump into each other before she finally breaks free. Bray's eyes narrow.

'What the hell was that?'

Garvan smiles quickly and clears his throat. 'Nothing. Why?'

Bray quietly stares at him for another minute before shaking his head. He looks around the living room, a lump forming in his throat at the thought of what they are giving up. Because of his arrival on Earth, they now have to leave the farm.

'I'll make this up to them. No matter what.'

Garvan places his hand on Bray's shoulder and squeezes it. 'They're not asking you to. This isn't down to you.'

'I know, it's just really shite, Garvan.'

'That's a pretty big understatement. It's their decision though.' He nods towards the mantle, now cleared of all photos. 'They have all the reminders they need. Besides, the great thing about memories is that they're portable. They're bringing Shayla with them for the ride.' He taps the side of his head. 'She'll always be up here.'

Bray smiles at him. 'You know, you really are a big softy under all that muscle.'

Garvan smirks at him. 'How about you say that again and I'll prove you wrong.'

Bray clasps his hands behind his head as he shuffles around the room. 'Between my brother issues and your problems with One, we're a right pair of trouble makers.'

Garvan laughs. 'Probably should get a health warning tattooed on our foreheads.'

'At the very least.' Bray drops his arms to his side as he looks around. 'I've had a lot of good memories here.'

'And some embarrassing ones if your haircut in those photos is anything to go by.'

Morgan appears at the doorway again and

unlatches a cupboard beside him to take out an unopened bottle of scotch. 'Bastards have taken enough. I'll be damned if they're getting this too.'

In spite of the sombreness of the moment, the men laugh. Morgan takes one last look around then, without another word, leaves the house.

Bray thumps Garvan in the arm. 'Let's get out of here.' Garvan throws his arm over Bray's shoulder as they walk down the back steps to the barn.

Morgan settles into the pilot seat. Even though Bray argued the point, repeatedly, Morgan insisted on piloting the shuttle himself. After spending all his life on the surface, he knows the best ways into the city without attracting too much attention. There's logic to his argument but that doesn't mean Bray is happy about it. Morgan spins his seat around to face Bray. 'We all set, Commander?'

Bray glances at Erin and Garvan, seeing a firm determination on their faces. 'Let's do this.'

∞

'Are you sure you want to do this?'

Garvan scowls over his shoulder at Bray.

Bray holds up his hands, surrendering to Garvan's stern expression. 'Fine. I'll back off.' Garvan walks back to Erin and the two go over their side of the plan again.

Bray leaves them to it, focusing on the view out the front window. Now that he's been in the shuttle with

Morgan for nearly an hour, he has to admit, Morgan was the best one to pilot. He knows the area better than Bray does.

Bray takes a few deep breaths to calm his stomach. They should get to the safe area outside the Council offices in an hour or so. It's not the breaking into HQ part of the plan that's worrying Bray. It's using Garvan as bait to figure out the location of the lab that's giving him reason to question their plan. Far too many uncertainties surround Garvan's part in the whole thing. They're counting on One's dislike of Garvan and that's not something they can plan on. One could very well just shoot him in the head.

He massages the corner of his eye, but instead of comforting, the irritating pain steps up a gear. Hopefully, once the adrenaline kicks in, it will mask the discomfort.

'You going to tell me what's wrong with that?'

Bray raises his eyebrow. 'With what?'

Morgan sighs and focuses out the window. 'You know what. I'm no fool, Bray. Is it serious?'

Bray responds with a half-hearted shrug. 'Don't know. Don't know much about it at all really.'

'You going to be okay to do this?'

'I'll be fine, really.'

Morgan glances at him briefly, not in the slightest bit convinced. To distract himself, he checks the sensors for the hundredth time. They've tested the Series-1 and its signal confused the new Foundation sensors. As far as they were concerned, it was an old land transport, nothing to look twice at. Bray just hopes the same happens as they get closer to HQ.

'He'll be fine,' Morgan says.

Bray wipes his clammy hands on the legs of his trousers. 'He shouldn't be doing this.'

Morgan glances back at Garvan and smiles. 'I'd like to see you convince him otherwise. It's his choice.'

'It just feels wrong. We shouldn't be handing him over.'

'You need a distraction to get you and Erin in. Garvan is the perfect one. They'll be keeping an eye out for him, so hopefully they won't be too focused on other areas of the base. It's your best chance, Bray. You know that.'

'Sounds good in theory, but what if they hurt him?'

'You're going to get me the hell out of there before that happens,' Garvan says from behind Bray. 'Besides, I survived two years in Tyrat. You saying I can't handle this?'

'Of course I'm not. I just don't trust the Foundation.'

Garvan smirks. 'Who does? Besides, what's to say I'm not going to be giving little Harvey—sorry, One, as good as I get?'

'You planning on getting in a few hits of your own?'

Garvan nods and rubs his hands together. 'Too damn right I am.'

'How do you know One won't just kill you?'

Garvan smiles, but there's no warmth in it. 'I know little Harvey. He'll want to gloat. He came all the way to Tyrat to make sure I knew he was behind what happened to me. He's not going to let a perfect opportunity like this pass by without a bit of an I-told-you-so moment.'

Bray nods but doesn't feel convinced.

∞

Morgan takes the ship down just outside the city limits. Erin steps on to the grass and peers around her.

'This okay for you?' Morgan asks.

She nods and points to the small group of derelict buildings to his right. 'It's the perfect place for a convict to hide out. Right, Garvan?'

Garvan joins her and nods. 'Looks good to me. Nice and homey. What was this place?'

'It used to be the livestock market. Once everything became automated, the skills dried up, people shifted to synthetic meat and this place crumbled. There must be half a dozen units like this one around the city limits.'

Garvan shakes his head. 'Another scar left by the Council. I'm surprised they haven't rezoned this area.'

'They've tried but no one wants to live somewhere animals were bought and sold,' Erin replies.

Garvan makes a face. 'If everyone had that

mentality, the Outer Sector would be deserted.' He swings his arms by his side. 'Right, time to get this show on the road. You sure a drone is due to pass over here soon?'

Erin nods. 'Of course I'm sure. I checked the schedule before we left. Just don't dance around in clear sight. It needs to appear authentic.'

Garvan snorts. 'Hey don't worry about my acting skills, Commander. I've been faking interest in whatever Bray says for weeks now.'

'Wait!'

Garvan spins to focus on Bray. 'That was a joke.'

'Yeah, I know that. Can I have a word with you? In private.'

'We've gone over this again and again. Time's getting on.'

Bray grips Garvan's arm and guides him around the back of the transport. 'Are you—'

'Yes, damn it!' Garvan runs his hands through his hair and takes a few deep breaths. 'Listen, I appreciate you're worried about me, but I've got this. I'm not going to do anything stupid. I'm not going to get myself killed, and I sure as hell don't want to be in there a minute longer than necessary. Now, will you get your ass back on the transport and let me get arrested in peace.'

Bray slaps Garvan on the shoulder then boards the ship again. He watches out the window as Garvan disappears into the nearest shed.

Bray lowers into the seat beside Morgan and rests

his foot on the console in front of him. He yelps as Erin thumps him in the arm. 'Hey, what the hell was that for?'

'You're staring after him like some sort of idiot. Toughen up. You're supposed to be a damn Hunter. Start acting like one. You're going into the building and are damn well going to take what you want. Then you're going to battle your way out, taking down as many Foundation security as possible, present company excluded of course, before rescuing Garvan and making a speedy get-away. From what I've heard about you Hunters, you've taken what doesn't belong to you hundreds of times. This time is no different. Got it?'

Bray smiles and nods. 'Got it, Commander.'

Bray shuffles in his seat, anxious to get moving.

'Will you quit squirming?'

Bray smiles apologetically at Erin. 'What's taking so long?'

She thumps him in the arm. 'Sit still and stop talking. Do you want to end up with a crooked face?'

Bray clamps his mouth shut and stares at the wall opposite him. He's dubious about how good the disguise will actually be. No matter what he does, an image of a bad nose and thick rimmed glasses continues to pop into his head. Erin has assured him numerous times over the last few minutes that the synthetic skin she is using is nearly impossible to tell from real skin.

The drones in and around HQ have face recognition built in. As long as they don't cross reference his face to that on a wanted list or prison record, it doesn't really matter what he looks like. The drones will log his face as unknown and it will be added to a register to be checked later. He plans to be well gone before anyone comes to have a chat with him.

Erin steps back and nods. 'I think that'll do.'

'Think?'

'It'll do.' She holds up a small mirror and Bray is surprised at the reflection facing him. Erin has somehow managed to make him appear like he's in his late forties to early fifties. The addition of some wrinkles under his eyes and on his brow, added with the grey flecks in his temples is simple yet effective. His nose is a different shape as is his chin, but the most noticeable transformation is his facial implant. It's completely gone.

'How'd you manage to hide my implant?'

She rests her hands on her hips, more than a little happy with herself. 'I used a thicker layer of synthetic skin to mask it. It won't pass up close. It looks like there's something trying to break out from under your skin, but from afar, it's convincing.'

'You can say that again,' Morgan adds as he joins them in the back of the transport. 'I barely recognise you.'

Bray stands up and slips his arms into the

Foundation jacket. 'That's the plan.'

Erin straightens his uniform, making sure it will pass as acceptable. At least this time the uniform fits and doesn't smell like the last one. 'Okay, you're ready. Best we get this over with. Your face won't hold up for long. I'd rather we were far from the drones before it begins to disintegrate.'

She gives her father a tight hug. 'Stay out of sight until we're ready.'

He rolls his eyes and gently jostles her towards the door. 'I know what I'm doing. Get out of here.'

Bray picks up the bag with their gear and follows Erin out the door.

'Hey.'

They both glance back at Morgan.

'Just make sure three of you come back. Got it?'

∞

Garvan paces his small cell. The sterile white room is hurting his eyes. The bright lights exploding from the ceiling seem to reflect off everything, even the polished surface of the bench serving as a bed. Give him the dingy darkness of Tyrat any day over this.

Footsteps echo off the bare walls of the corridor, heading in his direction. Adrenaline builds in his body and the hairs on the back of his neck stand to attention as the person approaches. He knows it's One on his way to gloat. He expected a visit before now. Perhaps Harvey was preening himself in the mirror to make sure everything was in place before he paid his prisoner a visit.

The man himself steps around the corner and stops in front of the bars. Garvan faces him, his shoulders back and his face blank. He doesn't say a word. Let Harvey make the first move. Even though the years in prison have altered Garvan's appearance, he still reckons he's fairing a lot better than Harvey.

His unmasked face is heavily lined, ageing him by a good ten to fifteen years. If Garvan didn't know any better, he'd put him in his late-seventies. His thinning, brown hair is scraped back from his face with at least half a bottle of gel to keep it in place. Either his heavy, velvet robe is adding pounds to his weight or Harvey has been enjoying the finer things in life a little too much. If this is what being the head of the Council does to you, Harvey can keep his position.

A few minutes of silence stretch on before One's shoulders drop slightly and he sighs dramatically. 'Well, I must say you are an unwelcome surprise. I had hoped the cameras in the hangar malfunctioned. It appears I am not that fortunate.'

Garvan smiles widely, but doesn't say anything.

'Nothing to say for yourself?' One paces in front of the cell, his robe trailing after him like a faithful companion. 'The years have changed you, Wade.'

Garvan steps up to the bars and gets a little kick of satisfaction when Harvey takes a step away. 'You too.' Garvan rests his hands on the top of the cell door and leans over. The smaller man's eyes focus on the large bulging muscles in Garvan's strained arms. Garvan smiles again. 'Council life suits you. You've grown into an impressive... specimen.'

A slight pink tinge touches One's face as he sneers up at Garvan. 'It seems shipping you to Tyrat has not had the effect on you I thought it would.'

'Sorry about that. I did consider lying down and dying, but I reassessed my situation. I thought it would be much more fun to survive and, hopefully one day, repay your hospitality.' Garvan holds his arms out to the side and smiles. 'How about a thank you hug?'

One steps back again and Garvan laughs—partly for show, but also partly because he's enjoying intimidating the most powerful man in the Council. 'What's wrong? Don't fancy stepping in here with me?'

'You know, it's funny, I thought losing your freedom, your career,' One smiles serenely, 'your family, would have stilted your spirit at least. If I had lost all that, I doubt I'd still be standing.'

At the mention of his family, Garvan's muscles tense.

'Oh, I see that struck a chord with you. Tell me old friend, do they enter your mind often?'

'I'd rate my cockroach cell-mates as old friends. You, not so much.'

'Deflecting again? You can't seriously tell me you're not even the slightest bit interested in them.

How about your wife, Celeste?'

Garvan barely manages to remain composed. Having a quarrel with the bars of his cell won't do much good.

'She was humiliated when you were arrested. Scorned by the neighbours, forced to relocate to escape the stares, escape the ridicule.'

'That's on you.'

One shrugs. 'As far as Celeste, your children, and everyone else was and still is concerned, you turned your back on them. Betrayed them. She had no choice but to remarry in order to resurrect some part of her life.'

Garvan shrugs, trying to appear nonchalant. 'That's Foundation law, you expected her not to obey?'

'She lived a fulfilled, happy life in the arms of another man,' One continues, ignoring Garvan's comment, 'From what I hear, she never mentioned you once. Your own children were forbidden to talk about their embarrassment of a father. They even changed their surnames to avoid your legacy.' One steps up to the bars. 'That's how much they hated you, Wade.'

'Will you shut up if I start crying?'

One pauses and pretends to seem upset. 'Now isn't the time for light-heartedness. I have some distressing news. Your wife died in a transport accident six months ago. I checked her records after her death. Do you know she went so far as to have someone erase you from her records? You don't exist in her life. Her new husband is listed as the father of your children. Now, you can't tell me that doesn't hurt.'

Garvan leans forward again and smiles even though he feels physically sick. 'Oh Harvey. Please stop, I can't take this anymore,' he forces the sarcastic reply out past the hollow feeling in his gut.

One thrusts out his chest. 'I should have killed you instead of making the mistake of sending you away.'

'You can't kill me.' Garvan lowers onto the rock hard bunk and clasps his hands on his knees. 'You see, if you kill me, you'll never know if I've kept your little secret.'

One's confident posture deflates almost as if someone had let the air out of him. He steps up to the bars and drops his voice. 'Who have you told?'

Garvan laughs at the panic in One's voice. 'I couldn't possibly say.'

One runs his fingers over the large gold medallion resting on his round stomach. 'You know, in my position, I can do a lot worse than kill you. You think Tyrat was bad. I can bury you in the most severe places in the galaxy. I can leave you to rot alone in the dark.'

Garvan shrugs. 'Been there, done that. C'mon, Harves, what else you got for me? You're Head of the Foundation Council. You really just going to leave me in the dark somewhere? Is that the best you can do?' He tuts and shakes his head slowly. 'I gotta tell you,

I'm a little disappointed.'

One is silent for a moment, then a sly smiles spreads across his face. He crosses his arms, tapping a chubby finger against his chin. 'I believe I may just have a use for a strong animal such as yourself.'

'Animal? Ouch. Now you're hurting my feelings.'

One's laugh is fake and laced with arrogance. 'I plan to do more than merely hurt your feelings. By the time I'm finished with you, you'll do everything I say.'

One storms away, his robe trailing behind him. As soon as the door at the end of the corridor shuts, Garvan shuffles back further on the hard bunk. Fully aware he's probably under surveillance, he doesn't let the anger, hurt, and sorrow flow from his body. He knew Celeste would move on, but he was hoping she would at least be a little sad to see him go. Hearing that she erased him from her life hurt more than he expected. Even though he was in prison and far from anyone that interested him in that way, he remained faithful to her and their marriage, which was more than she had done.

Losing his children upsets him more. He'd die for his son and daughter. They're the best thing he's ever done and they are ashamed and disgraced by him. That pisses him off more than anything.

He clenches his hands on his knees while he shoves his aggression deep down inside himself. Harvey took every bit of his life from him. He's got nothing to lose by tearing the man apart with his bare hands.

∞

Bray feels like all eyes are on him as he strides confidently through the main doors of Foundation HQ. He passes a cursory glance by the drones and is granted entry to the large atrium. His Commander uniform doesn't attract much attention, especially since he is walking side by side with a fellow officer. Bray does his best to keep in step with Erin as she weaves through the building. Using her keycode, she leads him through a set of enormous double doors and into a brightly lit corridor. Without a word, she continues down the corridor to the end door and ushers him inside.

Bray quickly checks each of the stalls in the bathroom and nods the all clear. 'Which one?'

Erin pulls a panel off the back of the door and programs an 'Out of Service' message to be displayed on the outside of the door. Once finished she locks it and faces him. 'Third from the left.'

As he gets to work separating the panel from the rest of the ceiling, Erin pulls off her uniform jacket, rolls it in to a ball and shoves it in to the disposal unit under the sink. Bray raises an eyebrow at her actions. Erin shrugs. 'It's not like I'll be needing it after today.'

'Listen, Erin. I can do this myself. There's no need to get you involved.'

She joins him in the cubicle. 'I'm already involved,

old man.'

Bray glances over at his reflection in the mirror and nods. 'I'll give you that one, just this once.'

She pulls a surveillance drone from her bag and makes sure her wrist unit is linked to its guidance and mapping system. Once satisfied, she passes it up to Bray who sets it down at the base of the vent. Erin launches the small drone and studies the base map on her unit. Bray watches as the robot disappears around the corner. 'You sure you know which way to send it?'

Erin sighs and gestures towards the vent. 'I'm not going to dignify that with a response. After you, Commander.'

Putting his trust in Erin, Bray heaves himself up into the vent, reaching down to pull Erin up after him. Erin concentrates on guiding the drone while Bray reseals the hatch, hiding their exit from below.

After waiting a few minutes in the cramped, chilly vent Erin finally nods. 'Okay. We've got the correct path. Ready?'

Bray nods. He's more than ready to get out of this tight vent. 'Go for it.'

16

Erin holds up her hand and Bray comes to a stop. She tucks her legs under her and points a gloved finger at the screen on her wrist. 'Garvan's transponder is on the move. He's heading our way quickly.'

Bray glances at the screen and the rapidly moving green dot. They've been crawling, scaling walls, and weaving through the ventilation system on the base for what seems like hours. Even though the surrounding air is chilled, Bray can feel the sweat trailing down his back. What he wouldn't give for a wide open space right about now.

He wipes his arm across his sweaty brow, picking

flakes of artificial skin from the material. His disguise is spread along the shafts from the bathroom to their current location. He dreads thinking what he actually looks like at the moment. 'Must be on the elevator.'

Erin tightens the strap of her gun. 'Yeah, and we're not.' She sits on the edge of the vent and peers into the depths below. 'If we're going to get there at the same time as him, we'll have to go a different route.'

Bray peers down the shaft and forces a smile on his face. 'Ladies first.'

Erin flashes him a smile, then presses her boots against each side of the vent. Keeping pressure on the soles of her feet, she shuffles down the tunnel, her hands pressed against the sides to steady her downward shuffle. Bray waits until she's a few paces below the edge before he joins her. The way Erin practically threw herself over the edge is making his need to pause a little ridiculous. He's never been good with heights, but it's not the time to let the fear take hold.

Bray shuffles after her, trying to focus as much as he can on his hands against the sides. After a few minutes, his muscles are screaming for relief. The tunnel isn't wide enough to extend his limbs fully, the awkward angle and the weight of his own body only adding to the discomfort.

'Hold up.'

Bray stops, locking his arms as much as he can to stop himself from landing on Erin and dragging her down with him. She checks the screen and smiles up at him. 'We're at the limit. It's about a twelve-foot drop after the defences. Once they drop the shield to bring Garvan through we'll have to drop the last bit.'

'No problem.' It's actually a big problem. Landing on legs that already feel like jelly is going to hurt.

'Bring back memories, huh?'

Bray looks down at Erin and remembers the same expression on her face when she was climbing the chimney with him. 'Bit bigger than your folks place.'

'You know, we should have tackled the chimney again, for old time's sake.'

'You really see the two of us fitting up there now?'

She shakes her head. 'No, I guess not. Would have been fun to try though. Okay, he's there. Ready to drop?'

'Just make sure you get out of the way so I don't land on you.'

'On three. One, two, now!'

Bray lets go. He hears Erin hitting the ground and braces for the impact. His own feet hit the bottom, his legs buckling from under him. He lies, groaning on the ground as Erin's face appears over him, her beaming smile visible in the dim light. 'That was fun. C'mon old man, get up.'

Bray rolls over to his side and forces his tingling feet to cooperate. 'Less of the old man stuff. I'm younger than you.'

She pats his cheek. 'Not quite acting like it right now.' She glances down at the screen then points her light into the tunnel to their right. 'This way and watch your head. It may get a little snug.'

∞

Snug is a nice way of putting it. Bray wriggles his arms from under his body and pulls himself forward again, then repeats the process. He thought the height in the tunnel was bad, but this is worse. Bray will face most things head on without blinking, but tight spaces are another force altogether. He's struggling to keep himself together, but losing it in this space will make things so much worse. All he can do is focus on the bottom of Erin's boots in front of him and keep going. He can freak out once he can stand up again. He's not ashamed of his fear. It's not something he had when he was a child. The Foundation were the ones who kindly gave it to him when he was their guest on Tyrat a few years ago.

To entertain themselves, the guards would throw two prisoners against each other. The prize was a badly needed plate of slop and all you had to do was kill the other prisoner to get it. Bray didn't hesitate to do exactly that. He was starving and needed the food. He had knelt in his opponents spreading pool of blood and watched as the greedy guards exchanged credits. He had earned them quite a bit of overtime pay in the space of a ten-minute duel. But, instead of getting his meal, Bray was punished for finishing the fight too quick. Bray had beaten the man to death. It was far from quick, but the guards disagreed and he had been dragged kicking and screaming into the isolation area.

Each punishment box, or 'crate' was a three-foot square windowless tomb. The guards could control the ventilation and sometimes decided Bray could do without a luxury like air. Food was indescribable slimy muck that tasted worse than the warm, rancid gas that passed for air when they decided he deserved it.

He spent three nightmare filled, hellish weeks in the crate until Avoca appeared one day and took him out of there. Ever since that day, small spaces and him did not get along. He'd challenge anyone to spend even an hour in a crate and not feel the same.

Erin's feet disappear and she bends down to peer back at him in the dark tunnel. She holds out her hand and pulls him out of the tight fitting space. Bray can't get to his feet fast enough. He stands tall in the large access cavity and forces his fists to unclench. Erin looks up at him.

'Hey, you okay? You're a strange colour.'

He manages a quick nod. 'Bit of a squeeze.'

Erin's brows drop but she doesn't say anything else. She slides her hand under his t-shirt and rubs her palm in circles on his bare back as she checks the map again. Whatever she's doing helps push any lingering queasiness away.

'Better?'

Bray nods, feeling more like himself again. 'Thanks.'

She reaches up and kisses him on the cheek. 'Don't mention it.' She directs the surveillance drone into the vent above them. 'Our little friend needs to go out there.'

Bray keeps his fingers crossed as the drone disappears through the vent and into the main body of the hidden lab. It will take a few minutes for the drone to map the area, so he leans against the wall and stares at the image on Erin's wrist. While he watches, the arms of the map spread out as the drone travels along the corridor.

Finally, Erin points to her screen. Instead of floating on a sea of blackness, Garvan's green transponder dot is sitting on a newly formed path thanks to the drone.

'Ready?' Bray asks.

Erin nods and Bray gives her a leg up. She silently dislodges the grid and slides it out of the way. After checking the coast is clear, Erin pulls herself through the hole and disappears from sight. The end of a rope drops through the hole and shakes to signal she's ready. Bray takes hold and uses the rope to scale the wall. He pulls himself through the tight space and hangs on to the side as he gets his legs out. He drops to the ground then hoists Erin up again so she can pull the vent across. Without a word they take their guns out and silently make their way down the corridor toward Garvan's signal.

Just like the inside of Infinity, *Alpha* is vast, clean and bright. No lurking in dimly lit corners on a

Foundation ship. The unpainted metal under their feet doesn't help to mask their footsteps. Bray takes the lead so Erin can concentrate on keeping an eye out for anything suspicious on the screen. She taps him on the left shoulder so he takes that side corridor. The air-conditioning chills his damp skin, but it's a welcome relief. Anything is better than being buried alive in a hot, airless, box.

He stops when Erin taps him in the centre of his back. She shows him the screen.

'He's in there.'

Bray slowly approaches the door and bends down to examine the lock. 'This has me stumped. You?'

Erin checks for herself then shakes her head. 'It's a top of the line lock. Code's probably changed every day.' She curses and ducks down. 'Someone's coming up the lab stairs.' She directs the drone towards the ceiling and rushes back along the corridor with Bray. They peer around the corner as a short, robed man steps through the door. He adjusts the mask over his face and straightens the large medallion draped over his stomach before gliding back along the corridor in the opposite direction.

Bray waits until he's gone before he speaks. 'Great. What now?'

Erin taps the side of her nose and gestures for Bray to follow her. They reach the door again and she points up. Bray follows her finger and smiles when he sees the small drone firmly wedged in between the door and its frame.

'As I said, I'm a girl of many talents.'

'Yeah, well right now I just want to get into that room. I'll pat you on the back later.'

Even before he's finished the words, Erin steps aside as the door opens fully. 'You were saying?'

Bray shakes his head and raises his gun as he slowly enters the room. He creeps over to the glass panel on the far wall. Bray peeks through the thick glass in front of him and is at a loss for words. When he thought the Foundation was launching the project again, he never imagined they would do it to the extent they have. The lab sprawled over the level below them is beyond any state of the art facility he's ever seen.

Erin sucks in a breath as she joins Bray at the window. 'My God...'

Bray shakes his head. 'They've already begun modifying people.' Bray swallows deeply when he sees the bloody rags and instruments. A single drone is cleaning up after the surgery.

Bray shakes himself out of his daze and steps onto the platform at the top of the stairs. As soon as Erin has him covered, Bray slowly walks to the edge of the platform and carefully peers into the laboratory below. The drone has left, taking the bloody instruments with it, leaving the lab deserted. He listens for any noises that might prove otherwise, but it's clear.

'Watch the door.'

Bray slowly descends into the lab. He makes his

way through the lines of machinery and empty gurneys. The hairs on the back of Bray's neck rise to attention. This place gives him the creeps. He checks his palm unit again. Garvan should be to his right. Keeping an eye out for any trouble, he creeps towards his destination. He rounds a corner and faces a large white door with a small window cut into it. Bray peers through the window. A team of half a dozen surgeons are busy inside, preparing instruments and checking monitors. On a small table next to the head of the gurney, Bray can see what looks like an ocular implant. It's much bigger than his, than Gryffin's even, but then he realises the section at the back must go inside the person's head. Bray rubs his own implant. He hopes he doesn't have all that metal inside his head. One of the surgeons steps away from the table and Bray's mouth goes dry. Secured to the gurney in the centre of the room is Garvan.

17

Bray forces his feet to move away from the door. He gestures for Erin to join him. She hurries down the stairs and silently makes her way through the equipment. 'What is it?'

'Garvan's in there. He's about to get a new metal eye.'

'How many with him?'

'Six. No weapons that I can see. He's unconscious and strapped down.'

'What's your plan?'

Bray shrugs. 'Burst in and take them all down.'

Erin nods. 'Simple yet effective. On three?' She deals with the lock then steps out of the way for Bray to step through first.

They position themselves back at the door and Bray mouths three. The door slides back, sending the surprised doctors scattering like rabbits. It doesn't take a lot of convincing to get them cooperating. In fact, Bray and Erin don't have to utter a word. The men and women huddle in the corner with their hands in the air. Bray glances over at Erin.

'That was a bit of a let-down.'

She makes a face. 'It's no fun when they give up without a fight.' She races over to Garvan and checks the monitors. 'He seems unhurt, but he's unconscious.'

'Can you check the systems outside? See what we have to do to get the data.' Bray faces the corner full of quivering doctors. 'Who's in charge?'

'You are,' one of the doctors answers from the back of the pile.

Bray rolls his eyes. Evolution has completely removed the backbones from Foundation members. 'I mean who's in charge of this procedure?'

The same man slowly raises his hand. Bray hauls him out from behind his wall of bodies and shoves him against the gurney. 'What's wrong with him?'

The doctor shakes his head. 'Nothing, just anaesthetised.'

'Unhook him.'

The man stares down at Garvan then at Bray's gun. 'But... he's dangerous.'

Bray raises his gun. 'So is this. Do it.'

The man fumbles with the controls but finally manages to get his fingers to cooperate. 'It's off. He should wake up soon.'

'Now unhook everything else.'

The man does as he's told. 'You're him, aren't you?'

'Who?'

'Him. I can't believe you're here. One said he wouldn't bring you to Earth.' The doctor frowns and glances over his shoulder at Bray. 'I don't understand. Why wouldn't he tell me you're here?'

'Who exactly do you think I am?'

'The prototype of course. I have to say, I've been eager to examine you.' The doctor's attention momentarily locks on Bray's gun and he fumbles with the monitor in his hand, nearly dropping it to the ground. 'Why is One letting you do this?'

Bray jams the gun into the man's forehead. 'I'm not the prototype and you will not be examining me, him, or anyone else. It's time you resign.'

Sweat beads on the doctor's forehead. He swallows deeply and forces a weak smile on his greying face. He finishes with the wires and slowly turns to face Bray. 'If you're not the prototype you must be one of the Outer Sector models then.'

'What the hell is an Outer Sector model?' The doctor clamps his mouth shut so Bray does a little more convincing with the barrel of his gun. 'I suggest you talk.'

'The other cyborgs the Scientist created. One had

Forty-Three program them to stay in the Outer Sector until ordered otherwise. You shouldn't be here.'

'You've got me all wrong, Doc. I'm not a cyborg and I'm sure as hell not programmable.'

'It is you who is mistaken.' The doctor laughs nervously. He gestures to the large screen on the wall high above them. 'That system monitors all the cyborgs I have in this facility. Each model with a programmable chip is picked up once they are within range so I can monitor their performance.'

'So?'

'So, the purple dots are all the cyborgs I have here going through the process. The lone green dot is a cyborg of similar design but not one of my creations. The system recognises it but knows the signal is foreign to the others.'

'You've lost me, Doc.'

'That dot is you. It's showing in the operating suite. I don't have an implant and I haven't done anything to your friend. It's you.'

Bray stares in horror at the small flashing green dot. The doc is right. It's showing in their location. He glances out the door and sees a row of beds in the room opposite them. Each bed is occupied. He doesn't need to check the patients to know they've had the Scientist's special treatment. He focuses on the screen again and sees purple dots in the room, each one marking one of the sleeping cyborgs.

Bray tries to hold his quivering arm steady. He wants to dismiss the doctor's claims as nonsense but something in the back of his mind stops him.

'You didn't know?'

Bray tightens his grip on the gun and glares at the man. The doctor whimpers and a dark stain spreads down the front of his scrubs. 'Please—'

'What's One going to ask them to do—the cyborgs in the Outer Sector?'

The doctor frantically shakes his head. 'I don't know. I'm only in charge of the new models. I swear I don't know. Are you going to kill me?'

'Not sure yet.'

Erin pokes her head around the corner of the room. 'I think we have a problem.'

'What?'

'These systems are above my knowledge. It'll take a few hours to even turn one of them on let alone copy all the data.' Something catches her eye behind Bray. He follows her eyes, seeing what caught her attention. About a dozen beds line the walls of the room behind him, each one occupied by a sleeping cyborg. He wanders from bed to bed. 'Notice anything?'

Erin doesn't respond so he looks at her. 'You okay?'

She licks her dry lips and shakes her head. 'I knew you were telling the truth. I mean, you have the implant. But...'

He squeezes her arm firmly and forces her to look at him. 'Hey, you need to stay with me, okay? I know it's a shock but we need to keep focused.'

Erin nods and finally drags her eyes away from the sleeping cyborgs. He gestures to the doctor. 'So, Doc, is that the cure for the implant malfunctions? Use women instead of men?'

The doctor stares up at Bray in shock. 'You know about the problems with the implants? Yes, yes, it is… Well, I believe it is the case. All the female models have survived. It's quite remarkable really.'

Bray's only response it to drive the butt of his gun against the man's head causing him to slump to the floor.

Bray steps over to the gurney and gently shakes Garvan. 'Hey, buddy, time to wake up.' Nothing happens so Bray tries again, a little harder this time. 'Garvan! Wake up!'

Garvan peeks out of one eye. 'Do you mind. I've had a traumatic day. Can I not just have five minutes to myself.'

Bray smiles and shakes his head. 'I thought I'd have to carry you out of here.'

Garvan opens the other eye and stretches. 'You? Now that I'd like to see.'

'Are you okay?'

Garvan's face loses its cheer. 'I'm in one piece. Had a nice chat with Harvey, but he's still alive… unfortunately.'

'Yeah, well you can come back and kill him once we have our own army to back us up. You okay to walk, there's company on the way.'

Garvan slides off the bed and stretches again. 'Bit

groggy but I'm good.'

Garvan, Erin and Bray stand in the top of the range lab and stare at the mammoth task ahead of them. Advanced is an understatement. Bray's never seen equipment like this anywhere in the Outer Sector. He tries to activate the nearest unit to him, but he doesn't even know how to turn it on. He pulls a hand through his hair as he slowly spins in the room.

What the hell was he thinking? There's no way he's going to be able to figure out the system, let alone copy the data and get off the ship before the Foundation catch on that something's wrong.

Bray freezes. That's it. They need more time. If they had the resources and no time constraints, they could figure it out. Keeping his gun trained on the room of doctors, he leans in to Erin and Garvan so the Foundation personnel won't overhear. 'We're taking her.'

Erin glances around the room. 'The female doctor? Why her?'

Bray shakes his head. '*Alpha.*'

Erin's face remains expressionless for a good minute before she frowns and shakes her head slowly. 'You have got to be kidding me?'

'Listen—'

Erin forces him back a step. 'No, you listen. There's only three of us. How exactly do you plan to take the flagship, huh? I mean, you've completely lost your mind, Bray. It can't be done.'

Bray tries to take her arm but she snaps it out of his reach. 'Over the last year, I've spent a lot of time on Infinity. Roman insisted we all know how Foundation ships work. Their flight systems are automated. It's possible for one person to fly her.'

'Yeah, maybe using the basic drive engines, but if you're planning on taking her anywhere at speed, you need a full crew.'

'We only need the drive engines.'

'The Foundation fleet will catch you before you leave orbit. Each Foundation ship has a transponder built in. They'll know where you are no matter where you go.'

Bray smiles as his confidence in his plan grows. 'I know how to turn it off. How do you think Infinity has evaded capture for so long?'

Erin blows out a breath and peers back into the room. Bray can tell she's wavering. 'I know it's an ambitious plan, but I think we can pull it off. This is the perfect time. There's hardly any crew on board. If we can make it to the bridge, we can lock her down.'

Erin glances over her shoulder at him and purses her lips. 'Engineering.'

'What?'

'Everything can be accessed from engineering... on the deck above this one.'

Bray places his hands on her shoulders and locks on to her eyes. 'We doing this?'

Erin looks up at Garvan. 'What about you?'

He shrugs. 'I've given up trying to argue with him,

especially when he has that look on his face.' He shrugs. 'What the hell, I'm game. We're in a whole pile of shit as it is, might as well make it a damn impressive one.'

∞

Bray readjusts his grip on the doctor's coat and forces the small man along the corridor ahead of him. Erin had locked the medics in a closet keeping one aside to join them on their trip. If his ambitious plan has any chance of working, they have to get to engineering quickly, which means abandoning the vents and keeping to the main corridors.

They reach the polished metal doors of the elevator and Bray shoves the doctor's face against the keypad. 'Code.'

The man fumbles with his sleeve, trying to free his trembling hand from the arm of the too-big lab coat. Running out of patience, Bray rips the sleeve from the coat and forces the man's limp hand against the panel. It takes him a few attempts to keep his palm still enough for the system to scan him, but finally the doors slide back. Bray throws the man in and examines the elevator controls.

Engineering is listed as the bottom deck on the elevator. Seems the Council are more worried about someone stumbling upon their secret lab than they are about their ship being taken. Bray pushes the pad and the doors slide shut. As the lift begins its assent, his implant sends a spear of pain through his head. Bray curses and shoves the palm of his hand against the implant, hoping the pressure will ease some of the pain. Erin pries his hand away, showing blood smeared on his palm. 'It's weeping from the corner of your eye. You okay?'

He nods although he's very far from okay. The pain is building, making it hard to ignore, but he's damned if the Foundation's work on him is going to stop him from taking this ship. He wipes the blood with his sleeve then turns his back on Erin, hoping she'll get the hint.

The panel lights up, showing they've reached their destination. The doors part and Bray swings around the corner, gun raised, but they seem to be alone. He gestures for the others to join him on the large platform overlooking the engineering room. *Alpha*'s six main engines take up the centre of the five story room. Banks of computers and monitors service each engine. Another control station sits to the front of the room in front of a large viewscreen.

Bray cautiously approaches the edge of the two story high window and peers out. From this height, the view over the cargo hold is impressive. He smiles as he focuses on the area directly ahead of the ship. Even more impressive is the fact the enormous bay doors are open, showing blue cloudless sky outside. He smiles to himself. This plan may actually have a chance of working.

Garvan stands behind Bray and shakes his head. 'I

don't understand. Why is there a porthole here?'

Erin finishes securing the doctor to the railing running around the edge of the room before she answers, 'In emergencies, the ship can be fully operated from here: guidance, comms, engines, life support—everything. The engine room is the heart of the ship after all. It makes sense everything could be operated from here if needed.'

Bray examines the vast room. 'Which operating system wins out: command deck or engineering?'

Erin grins. 'Engineering, but we still need to lock down the command deck. If anyone gets in there, they could cause problems.'

Bray drops down through the railing, landing on the floor underneath. 'First things first, transponder.' He pictures the engineering deck on Infinity, trying to place the image over his current surroundings. Apart from the obvious size difference, the general layout of the deck is exactly like Infinity. He follows his memory to the far side of the room. Only the captain on each ship knows the location of the transponder, but if he's learned anything, it's that the Foundation are creatures of habit. Even their new cyborgs are based on Gryffin's design.

He runs his hand over the panel above the small unit shadowing engine number three. Bray wipes blood from his vision, but every time he clears his eye, it fills up again. 'Garvan. I think this is it.'

Garvan grabs a tool-kit from under one of the units and removes the panel. He smiles and points to a red box, firmly fixed to the wall. 'What do I do with it?'

Bray leans back on the unit behind him and squeezes his eyes shut. The pain is battling for control over his thoughts, and he's running out of strength to fight it. 'Open the box and remove the forth red control chip from the second line of components.'

Bray breaths steadily through his mouth as his stomach lurches. He's trying damn hard but is struggling to ignore the pain from his implant.

'Got it.'

'Now do the same with the tenth one on the last row. Swap the two chips and replace them. It should fool the ship in to thinking the system is still working, but the transmissions to HQ will stop.'

Erin shouts in triumph from the control panel on the top level. 'Bray, you're a genius. We've gone dark.'

Garvan places his hands on Bray's shoulders. 'Hey, you're looking rough.'

Bray snorts. 'Feel it too.' He forces his eyelids apart and glances up at Garvan. 'Do I want to know?'

Garvan's face grows serious as he leans forward to check him. 'Damn it, Bray. Your left eye, it's blue. All blue. It looks a bit like Gryffin's.'

Garvan's words echo in Bray's head. 'You mean artificial?'

Garvan shrugs. 'I'm far from being an expert but yeah. Not exactly like his, but I swear I can see robotic sections like Gryffin has.'

18

One remains silent as he calmly strides along the corridor to an empty office two doors down from the meeting room. Not for the first time he's grateful for the mask concealing his features. He seriously doubts he's hiding the raging anger from his face. Being summoned out of a Council meeting by Leeson can only mean one thing—trouble.

One waits until the door secures behind Leeson before he releases his frustration. He slams his palms down onto the desk and glares at Leeson. 'What could possibly be so important that you would bring me out of a Council meeting!'

Leeson takes a step back, stopping when his back

bumps against the door. 'I apologise, sir, but it is an emergency.'

One leans against the desk and crosses his arms. 'And...?'

Leeson wrings his hands together and focuses on the floor in front of him. 'Sir, I'm not sure how it happened—'

One rises to his feet. 'Just spit it out.'

'Sir, it's *Alpha*. She's been breached.'

One hears the words but struggles to absorb them. 'Impossible.'

'Internal sensors are showing activity in engineering. We're also getting no response from the lab.'

'Well why the hell are you standing here? Get the cyborgs in there. Now! If anything happens to the ship, I am holding you responsible.'

'Sir, there's more.'

One groans to himself. 'Care to enlighten me?'

'The prisoner, the one you sent for modification.'

'What about him?'

'He's on *Alpha*.'

One dismisses Leeson with a wave of his hand. Leeson stumbles from the room, shouting into his radio as he runs. Ignoring his brothers and sisters waiting in the room down the corridor for his return, One storms towards his office. He hurries over to his private elevator and steps inside. He pauses for a moment before pressing in the code for *Alpha*. The lights flash but blink red as a message displays on the screen: cannot access *Alpha.*

One grinds his teeth and tries again, but receives the same reply. He glares at the blinking message and shouts out, forcing his fist against the panel. This is because of Wade Garvan. He has no doubt about that. Somehow, he escaped the lab and took the ship. He should have stayed and watched as he was dissected.

He storms out of his elevator and slowly sinks into his seat. He'd give the cyborgs one chance to access *Alpha.* While he's less than thrilled about destroying the ship, he'd rather she was scrap than in the hands of that man.

One leans back in his chair and scolds himself. This is Wade Garvan he's talking about. The man was an architect, not a pilot. He seriously doubts the convict earned the necessary flight experience while at Tyrat. One shakes his head at his over-reaction. One pesky convict is no match for *Alpha*'s flight controls. Surely he has nothing to worry about.

∞

'We may have a problem,' Erin shouts from the upper level.

Garvan helps Bray to his feet. 'Seriously, Erin, we could do without you finding problems at every turn.'

Bray leans over, using the back of her chair as a support to keep him upright. He looks at the viewscreen in front of her. A group of cyborgs are approaching the ship fast. Erin runs her finger over the control system in front of them.

'C'mon! Where are you?' Her fingers speed over the controls, tapping furiously, much quicker than Bray can keep track of. 'Right, that should stop them. I've set the force field up around the cargo doors. It'll stop anything else from joining us.'

'You know the controls?'

Erin shakes her head at Bray. 'Security, remember. I was given a quick run through of force fields, etc. Anything that can be used to lock the ship down. Garvan, you and I have to secure the ship, sealing everything as we go. Who knows how many crew are still on board. We have to make sure they stay out of the way.' She unfastens a tall locker near the door and pulls a Foundation issue gun out for herself and Garvan. She passes him some rounds and loads more into her pocket.

'I'll head towards the command deck. You take the cargo hold. Meet in the middle. Bray, get her off the ground, now, before we have larger, better armed company.'

Without waiting for a response she leaves the room with Garvan running after her. Bray concentrates on the flight control and takes a deep breath. His eye still hurts like he's been bashed with the butt of a gun, but it's not as distracting as it was. He lowers into the seat and examines the panel. Like the rest of engineering, the flight controls are nearly a match to those on Infinity. He holds his breath and keys in the sequence that should activate her drive engines.

He completes the sequence and waits. A few seconds later he's rewarded by a gentle hum from behind him. He smiles as the sound builds when the two smaller drive engines power up. Feeling a little more confident, he runs through what to do next. He locates the controls that deal with navigation and his fingers hover over the panel. If he gets this right, *Alpha* should take off. If he gets it wrong, he could crash their escape route into the cargo bay floor. He holds his breath as he activates the controls, but nothing happens. A message flashes up on the screen in front of him: secure cargo ramp before take-off.

'Damn it.' He activates his radio and waits until Garvan finally answers. 'Where the hell are you?'

'Bit busy here mate.'

'She won't take off unless the ramp is closed.'

'Hate to state the obvious, but maybe you should close the ramp.'

Bray sighs. 'Thanks for the advice, but it won't shut until it's clear from personnel.'

Garvan is quiet for a few seconds. 'Understood. I'll go sweep the decks. Be ready to get out of here as soon as you can.'

Bray signs off and focuses on the screen showing the feed from the cargo bay. He hopes Garvan can handle the cyborgs. If he can't, they're stuck here.

∞

Garvan peers around the corner then pulls back quickly. Three very attractive women are approaching his direction along the corridor. They may be good looking but the fact they have glowing purple eyes is a bit of a turn off.

He checks his gun again, confirming it's still fully loaded. Killing has never been top of his to do list. While at Tyrat, he was forced to take the lives of six fellow inmates and he deeply regrets every single death. When put in a kill or be killed situation, self-preservation will overrule any moral issue he may have. If he has to kill these women, he'll do it—no question.

Garvan crouches down, pulls his knife from his belt and waits until the group approaches. As the shadow of the first woman reaches the corner, Garvan leaps out. He jams the knife into her neck while he shoots the next one in the head. With lightening quick reflexes, their final companion retaliates, striking at him with her metal fist. Garvan drops to the ground, yanking the knife out of first woman as he rolls away. He surges to his feet, gun raised and fires at the last cyborg. She ducks under the shot, spinning and kicking out at his chest with such force he slams into the wall behind him. Garvan gasps for breath, unable to side-step quick enough to avoid her metal hand clamping around his neck. She forces him up the wall, his feet dangling off the ground. Her hand tightens around his neck and his vision swims as he runs out of oxygen.

Just before he loses consciousness, he realises he still has the knife in his hand. Using what little energy he has, Garvan raises his hand. The cyborg's focus is on his face so she doesn't notice his hand rising and settling behind her head. Garvan tightens his grip then screams as he rams the knife into the back of her head. The light from her artificial eye glows bright, then flickers twice before dying. She drops Garvan to the ground and lands in a heap under him. Garvan rolls off the body and lies on his back gasping for breath.

As much as he'd like to lie on the floor and recover, he can't. Garvan pushes to his feet, steadying himself against the wall while his vision clears. He glances down at the bodies on the ground and shakes his head. 'Damn shame.'

He takes a deep breath then continues towards the cargo hold, locking down the side corridors as he goes. He finally reaches his destination, crouches down behind a crate of medical supplies and peers around the side. Another four women are standing in the cargo hold. The large ramp is still dropped but the rounds being fired in from outside bounce harmlessly against the shield Erin erected.

Garvan slowly stands up and rolls his shoulders. If he has to go out fighting these women so be it. Not many people can say they were taken down by a group of attractive cyborg women. He grins to himself. There are worse ways to go.

∞

Erin reaches up on her tip-toes and slips the panel off the vent servicing the command deck. HQ sealed off the bridge remotely at the first sign of trouble but that doesn't mean she still can't access any personnel that may still be inside. She slips the small drone in and watches on her monitor as it makes its way to the main room. She smiles to herself as the camera on the drone scans the room. It's empty.

Satisfied, she calls the drone back then works her way along the corridor, sealing any sections of corridor she can. Once locked down, the doors can only be unlocked from engineering. She steps around a corner and comes face to face with a tall, well-built woman. A cyborg woman.

Erin freezes, unable to get her mind to focus on anything other than the fact there's a real-life cyborg in front of her. An image of Daegan covered in metal springs into her mind, twisting her stomach.

Anger races to the surface, replacing the momentary shock at seeing a cyborg. Erin releases a shot but is a split second too slow. The woman's round slams into her side, knocking her to the ground. Erin scrambles to her feet and returns fire, keeping her body hidden around the corner. Adrenaline helps to mask the pain but it's not stopping the blood loss. If she doesn't patch herself up soon, she'll bleed out. Erin's continues firing as she searches in her pocket for the controls for the drone. She finally wraps her fingers around the controls.

The small drone won't be able to fire but it can do something just as useful. Erin watches on the screen as the drone approaches the back of the cyborg and flies straight into her. The cyborg pivots giving Erin the chance she needs. She spins around the corner, both guns in her raised hands. Erin empties the weapons into the cyborg's head, spraying bits of brain and component across the corridor.

Satisfied the woman isn't getting up again, she reloads her guns and tears her sleeve off. She rolls the material up and secures it to her side using her belt. It's not perfect but it'll have to do.

Erin pats the drone on the top and continues down the corridor.

19

Garvan presses his back to the crate and takes his first shot. Luck is on his side. It hits home, taking the side of the nearest cyborgs head off, her long blonde locks smeared with crimson. Without waiting for the others to catch on, he targets the next. The second in-between shots was enough time for the rest to react. A round punches through his upper arm, rendering it useless. Garvan switches his gun to the other hand and continues firing, but the women have taken cover.

'Stop wasting time. Surrender and hand over the ship.' The leader's voice is soft and timid, nothing like the deadly killer it came out of.

'You first, sweetheart.'

'You fail to understand, you will die.'

'Shucks, we've just met and you want to kill me already? I'm hurt.'

'I plan on killing you, not hurting you.'

He cracks his neck and smiles widely. 'Maybe, but I'm not going alone. Now, which of you fine ladies care to keep me company on the way?'

The only response is a shot that barely misses his head. Garvan throws himself around the other side of the crate, catching one of the women off guard. She may have a computer in her head, but the brown-haired woman's logic is flawed. She's keeping her eyes solely focused on one spot at the side of the crate. Her reward is a round to the side of her implant. The cyborg's head rocks back as the round strikes home. Blood explodes from the back of her head as sparks dance over the ruined implant and she collapses to the ground.

'Fancy changing your mind?' Garvan doesn't expect her to agree. He quickly manoeuvres closer to the cargo ramp and around the side of the two remaining cyborgs.

'Surrender.'

He shakes his head. Clearly, she's a woman of few words. Personally, he'd prefer someone a little chattier. When he finally finds the crate he was searching for, he activates as many of the surveillance drones as he can then grabs the master control from the side of the box. He sends the drones out of the box, not caring where they go as long as they offer some form of distraction.

The machines burst out of the box, and fly in the opposite direction towards the two remaining cyborgs. Using them as cover, Garvan hurries around the back of the women, getting right up behind one of them as she targets the flying robots. Garvan places a round in the back of her head and steps around the box to face the leader. She smiles at him, holstering her gun.

'I'm Nova.'

Garvan nods. 'I'm happy for you.'

She tears the weapon from his hands before he can react. After crushing the barrel in her hand she tosses it over her shoulder. Nova smiles which just makes her seem more menacing. Garvan doesn't have much experience with cyborgs. He only saw a few in passing on Tyrat when the Foundation brought them in to control the crowd. His main contact was with Gryffin, and that was reserved to a few minutes with him. Garvan isn't ashamed to admit that the Nomad leader scared the hell out of him. He knows Gryffin must have a softer side to have attracted and held on to someone like Terra, but he's damned if he can see it. Nova is just as intimidating as the Gryffin, probably more so because her voice is deceptively soft.

Garvan and Nova face each other in the centre of the cargo hold. Flashes of light illuminate the hold as the rounds bounce off the shielding. Apart from the crates lining the sides of the room, there's plenty of clear space in the middle for them to dance.

Garvan rolls his shoulders, using the time to examine his opponent. Nova drops her jacket to the floor and kicks it aside. Clearly this woman means business. The sleeveless t-shirt she's wearing is tight fitting, highlighting the metalwork on her chest. She clenches her metal fist, the muscles in her upper arm tensing as she tightens her grip. Her glowing purple eyes are solely focused on him and him alone. He's sure of one thing, he's in serious trouble.

'Are you ready?' she asks in her sweet voice.

Garvan smiles and shakes his arms. 'Don't hold back.'

She smiles back at him, baring her teeth. 'Never.'

Garvan calls her forward with a flick of his finger. 'I'm all yours.'

Nova rushes at Garvan. He dips and weaves right as she is about to reach him and slashes downwards with his knife. Nova sidesteps to the right and his blade passes a hair's breath from her face.

Before Nova can respond with a follow-up, Garvan swiftly punches her in the solar plexus. The blow knocks the wind out of the cyborg, stunning her, but not for long enough. Her alterations give her added strength and stamina above a normal human.

Garvan risks a quick glance to his right. The brawl has taken them dangerously close to the edge of the ramp. He knows things can't penetrate the shield from outside, but that's not the case from inside. If they get too near, he could find himself stuck in the

HQ hangar with a pissed off cyborg. She needs to leave but he'd prefer to stay on board if he can.

Nova smiles and rushes him again. If she wants to keep going, Garvan is only happy to oblige. He sends a powerful sidekick into the cyborg's stomach, doubling her over. Before she can straighten, Garvan follows with a quick uppercut that throws her back a few steps.

She catches him by surprise, retaliating with a blow of her own. Her metal fist cuts into the side of his face, bouncing his brain around his skull. He shakes his head, trying to realign everything. Spitting blood on the floor, he roars and swipes at her legs, catching her in the shins with the full force of his legs. She tumbles to the ground, banging her head off the floor. Garvan slides across the floor towards her. He flattens his body out, approaching her feet first. Instead of striking her, Garvan wraps his feet around Nova's neck.

The manoeuvre catches her off guard. Nova stares at Garvan, her eyes wide in surprise. He tries to grab her metal hand but she is too quick. The blow to his groin turns his legs to jelly. She twists out of his grip, then vaults to her feet, grins savagely and kicks out with her boot. Garvan rolls to the side, narrowly avoiding a serious headache.

Nova's leg smashes into the floor, denting the smooth metal surface. Garvan rolls to his feet, anger taking over completely. He's been in enough life and death situations to know it's time to take this to a new level. Woman or not, Nova has to die. Garvan spins his body around, sweeping his foot towards his opponent's head. The attack is so quick the blow propels her off her feet and into the air.

She lands chest first on a stack of crates. Garvan rushes her from behind, and double punches into Nova's back. Air rushes from the cyborg's lungs as she is driven harder against the crates.

Bray's voice echoes in his ear. 'Running out of time, Garvan.'

He doesn't bother responding. Garvan glances past the cyborg. The edge of the ramp is just an arm's length away from her now. His attention goes back to Nova. There's no way she's going to back down. She'll keep going until there's nothing left. Garvan may be a good fighter but she will win. He knows that. She must have a few broken ribs and a concussion, but isn't showing any discomfort.

Garvan glances down at the ground again and blows out a long breath. There's only one way to get her off the ramp and it involves him personally escorting her. He made a promise he'd repay Bray for saving his life. This might just be his chance.

He straightens, wincing as his own cracked and broken ribs protest. 'Hopefully, this is going to hurt you a little more than it's going to hurt me.'

Nova tilts her head to the side, unsure what he is talking about.

Garvan shouts and barrels into Nova. He grabs the cyborg around the waist and throws them both off the edge of the ramp. He twists in mid-air, putting her body between him and the ground. If he's going down, he might as well have a semi-comfortable landing.

Nova collides with a transport loaded with cargo crates under *Alpha*'s ramp. Her body makes a painful cracking and crunching sound as the wooden and plastic crates shatter under the enormous pressure from both bodies landing on them.

Garvan tries to separate himself from the unconscious cyborg, but judging by the angle of his arm, it's seriously broken. It also doesn't help that a large piece of plastic has pierced Nova's stomach and penetrated his side, pinning them together.

'That's got to hurt you more than it hurts me.' He pats Nova on the face. 'Cheers for the soft landing,' Garvan mutters to himself.

He tilts his head up, smiling as he watches *Alpha*'s ramp lift, sealing her underside from the troops firing in from the hangar. The enormous vessel slowly rises off the ground and crawls towards the exit, the roar of her engines deafening inside the domed space. In spite of the situation, Garvan laughs.

'Trust you to do the impossible, Bray.' He nods to the guards as they surround him and the unconscious cyborg. 'You seem to have lost something.' He's still laughing as one of the guards bashes him on the head with the end of his gun, knocking him out.

∞

Bray glances at the camera targeting the loading ramp of *Alpha*, watching in horror as Garvan and a cyborg tumble from the edge of the ramp onto a transport below. His first instinct is to stop *Alpha* and go back for him, but Erin stops him. She places a bloody hand on his and shakes her head. 'We have to go. If we stop now, we're all dead.'

Bray's hands still want to stop the ship but the truth of her words somehow breaks through. He accelerates, propelling *Alpha* further out of the base. Her powerful drive engines carry her through the doors, past countless transports, each one firing on her. She barely feels the impact. Her shields and sheer size means their attack is useless. One may have wanted to destroy the ship, but there's nothing on the base powerful enough to actually do the deed.

Bray watches in the rear screen as a swarm of security surround Garvan, hiding him from view. His fingers hover over the weapons console. He'd give anything to raze the base to the ground but not with Garvan inside. Instead, he targets the transports lining the courtyard outside. It won't stop the Foundation from retaliating but reducing the ships to scrap metal makes him feel a whole lot better.

'Cloaks... ' Erin mutters from her position on the floor.

Bray tears his eyes from the back of the ship and identifies the cloaking controls. He hides the Foundation flagship from view, both visually and electronically. Even though they managed to carry out the impossible, the victory means nothing. He left Garvan behind.

20

It takes Bray a good five minutes to convince Morgan they have control of *Alpha*. Even when they temporarily uncloak over the coast to load the transport, Morgan still finds it hard to believe. His uncle had been less than happy about the new plan but they had finally talked him into meeting at the coast about two hours from the base. It took *Alpha* about twenty minutes to make the same journey. Bray spent every minute of the time checking sensors, sure the Foundation would appear at any moment.

When his uncle finally reached them, his anger over what happened to Erin over-shadowed his feelings about *Alpha*.

'You stupid girl. Why'd you go and get yourself shot?'

She smiles, but it's not her usual full grin. 'Sorry, Dad, it wasn't planned.'

Morgan unfastens her makeshift bandage, replacing it with a better one from a med kit Bray found.

Bray checks his gun, and stuffs it back in its holster. 'You see to Erin. Everything is locked down and the ship is cloaked. The Foundation won't be able to detect you.' He pulls himself up onto the platform to the upper deck.

'Now you hold on there one minute. Where exactly do you think you're going?'

'I have to go back for him.'

Morgan rises to his feet and shakes his head. 'No, you do not.'

'Morgan, I said I have to go back! I'm not leaving here without him.'

'Hell yes you are. Now you listen here, Brayden Sawyer. At the moment, we are sitting over a beach on the Foundation's flagship complete with state of the art torture laboratory. If you think my daughter and Garvan went along with your hair-brained plan just so you could give up and hand it all back, you're sorely mistaken.'

'And if you think I'm leaving without him, you're sorely mistaken.'

'He'd want you to go,' Erin mutters from the

ground.

Bray looks down at her. Her eyes are unfocused but her voice is clear and loud.

'I don't give a damn what he wants. We can't just leave him there. They'll kill him! We don't leave people behind.'

'And we don't put everyone's lives at risk by going back into the enemy stronghold,' Erin whispers. 'Garvan knew full well what he was doing. Don't you dare disrespect his sacrifice by getting yourself killed. He gave his life for yours. The least you can do is respect that and not do something bloody stupid, no matter how much we all want to. Garvan means something to each of us. You think I want to leave him behind? Well, I don't, but right now, we don't have a choice.'

Bray beats his fist against the wall. 'He won't have to sacrifice anything if I go back!'

Morgan grabs Bray by both shoulders and manhandles him down the steps. He shoves him into the pilot seat and holds him down by the shoulders. Morgan points to the floor at his feet where Erin is lying with blood seeping through her bandages. 'Garvan and Erin put their necks on the line to save yours. To save all of our lives. Erin is right. Show both of them the respect they deserve. Garvan isn't dead yet, but if Erin keeps bleeding out like that she will be. I've already lost Shayla, I can't lose her too. We have to go now.'

Bray looks down at Erin and the truth of Morgan's

words hits him. By going back for Garvan, he risks killing them all. It's a selfish decision and one Garvan would definitely disapprove of. 'Can you get your hands off me?'

Morgan slowly lifts his hands and watches as Bray swivels around in his seat. Bray pulls up a chart and confirms the co-ordinates before moving *Alpha* away from the beach.

'How is she?' Bray asks Morgan as he crouches beside his daughter.

'Unconscious. I need to stop the bleeding.'

'How bad is it?'

'Through and through.'

'Makes things easier.'

'Yeah, also makes for two wounds.'

Morgan gets up and searches under a few of the consoles. He reappears a moment later with a small blue metal case. He examines the contents of the kit then takes two silver discs from the case, dropping the other four to the floor.

He slides his hand under her body again, pressing one of the discs against her skin. He hears a faint hissing sound then repeats the process with the wound on her back.

Bray watches in amazement as the disc fuses itself to her skin, sealing the wound. 'What are they?'

Morgan examines his work as he answers, 'New type of field dressing. She finally convinced me to upgrade our med kit a few weeks ago. I wasn't keen on these new-fangled toys. Glad I let her convince me otherwise. They expand into the wound, locate the damage and repair it.'

Bray's eyebrows shoot up. 'Seriously? In the Outer Sector a field dressing is just that—a roll of bandage.'

Morgan wipes his hands on his trouser legs. 'It's only temporary. She still needs proper medical attention.' Morgan brushes damp hair from her face. 'Just hang on in there. I'll get you help. I promise.' He drapes a blanket over Erin, and joins Bray at the helm.

'Bray?'

He glances over his shoulder at Morgan. 'Yeah?'

'You know where to take her, right?'

Bray forces a smile on his face and nods. 'Trust me.'

∞

One straightens his robes and runs a hand over his hair, smoothing it back in to place. He glances around the ruined remains of his office and finally locates his chair beside the far wall. He stumbles over the piles of books in his way, grabs the chair by the back and hauls it over the destruction. One clears a space behind his desk, kicking the debris aside with his foot. Once there's enough room, he places the chair in its rightful spot and lowers into it. He transmits a message to housekeeping, demanding they report to his office in one hours' time, then clasps his hands together on his stomach and surveys the mess. His mess.

It's been years since he lost his temper like that. He thought he had complete control of himself, but after hearing about Wade and the other blasted rebels, he needed to unleash a little of the fury before it consumed him. He knew he should have stayed with Wade while he was being operated on. His weak stomach shouldn't have kept him from ensuring the punishment was carried out.

Then again, if he had stayed, he'd more than likely be trapped on *Alpha* as his prisoner. He's not angry about the loss of personnel or cyborgs. The lives mean nothing to him. He can always acquire more to take their place.

An hour before they attacked, fifteen fully operation cyborgs had been relocated to another area of the facility, including Nova. It was a lucky and well-timed decision. The loss of the lab and the doctors is a great hit to their cause, but irrational or not, the thing that's irritating him more than anything is the fact that Garvan fled with his ship.

The timid architect wasn't meant to survive the prison and become this muscled moron and he sure as hell wasn't meant to come back to Earth—ever. He didn't even get to properly question Wade before he escaped. He has no way of knowing if his secret is still a secret or if Wade had told every rebel and cyborg in the Outer Sector. He doubts anyone in the Foundation would believe or put merit in the word of a convict, but he isn't willing to stake his reputation or his life on it. Being in possession of the knowledge, Wade had power over him. He's One. No one in the Sector should have power over him, let alone Wade.

A neatly stacked pile of documents on the corner of his desk gets his attention. In anger he swipes his arm out, sweeping everything to the ground.

A knock sounds on the secret door to his office. Grumbling under his breath, he crosses the room and keys in the code to unlock the panel. A cyborg steps into the room, her face expressionless as she surveys the destruction he caused.

'What is it?'

'Nova is unconscious but should recover. She will need some additional work to restore her components. The prisoner is being treated. It is unknown if he will survive.'

'Prisoner? Why would I care about a prisoner?'

'Leeson said I should tell you. It's Wade Garvan.'

One slumps back against his desk, his hands gripping the edge to stop himself sliding to the ground. 'I don't understand. I was led to believe he escaped on *Alpha*.'

'Leeson contacted you when we apprehended him.' She glances over at his unit in pieces on the floor. 'You didn't get the message.'

'Clearly I didn't. Was he left behind?'

'He fought with Nova in the cargo bay. They were both knocked from the ship before it took off.'

One laughs loudly, not believing his luck. Just when he thought his future was unsure, the idiot waltzed back into his custody again. 'Perfect. Make sure no one speaks to him. Lock the entire med bay down. I am the only one with access to him, understand?'

'Yes, sir.'

He raises an eyebrow as he glances sideways at her. He's probably imagining it but he swears he caught a slight irritation in her tone. 'Leave one of your team with him at all times. Dismissed.'

She nods and without another word disappears through the door, closing it behind her.

Feeling slightly better about his predicament, he pushes to his feet and makes his way over to the window. It seems Nova and her team have already proved their worth. It will take a few weeks for the secondary lab to be made ready. That will give him time to obtain a new doctor and new subjects to alter. He'll make sure the task is taken care of without involving the rest of the Council. They may agree with the project, but they do not have as much invested as he does. The loss of *Alpha* will be a hard enough pill to swallow.

And he still has his trump card in the Outer Sector. The prototype. He may have told his brothers and sisters that Thirty-Five is not vital to their project, but that was a lie. Without the prototype, they can never hope to rectify the issues with the male subjects. Having an army of female cyborgs is an achievement, but having a male one would be quite a bonus. Besides, a part of him would like to have the prototype back on Earth. Something about the cyborg intrigues him. His defiance and continued stubbornness, in spite of all they put him through, fascinates him.

The prototype would undergo a complete rework. Millions of credits would not be wasted again. This time, One would make sure the control implant could not be overridden by anyone. There's no point having invested that much in a weapon if you then give it free will to do whatever it wants. No, he would correct that problem once and for all.

He is mere weeks away from officially being the greatest leader the Foundation has known, well, once *Alpha* is recovered. His cyborgs will take over Ultar, which, in turn, will weaken the opposition in the Outer Sector. With no defences left, they will submit to his rule. The colonists will provide everything the elite need thus ensuring survival of the most important people on Earth.

He smiles and hums to himself as he lowers into his chair. Having both the prototype and troublesome Wade modified to the new specification will give him two powerful bodyguards. With them at his side, fighting for him, he'd be unstoppable.

∞

Morgan releases his grip on Erin's arm as they approach their coordinates. So far, the journey from Earth has been uneventful. Between the lack of transponder and her cloaks, *Alpha* had managed to pass all defences unnoticed—for now. Just because they made it this far doesn't mean they will get away. Until they are safely at their destination, all bets are off. The increase in the number of ships surrounding Earth was obvious, but without anything to target, it was all for show. The modification the Council made to keep *Alpha*'s contents top secret proved useful in keeping her hidden.

The space station they are heading for is home to Evie and Felix Dixon, two of the most eccentric people he's ever met. After Avoca broke him out of Tyrat all those years ago, he took him to the station for recuperation and training. The Dixon's are long-time friends of Avoca and offered Bray somewhere to call home until he left to join *Perses*. The Dixon's managed to live right under the noses of the Foundation Council for many years. Bray isn't entirely sure what the couple do to survive out here, but he does know black market trading is top of the list. If you want something illegal, the Dixon's can get it for you—at a price of course.

Morgan frowns as he peers out the window. 'You sure this is a good idea?'

'The Dixon's will help her.'

Morgan nods, his expression grim. 'You're placing a lot of faith in these people. Are you sure they'll be accommodating?'

'I'm sure. We'll be safe here.'

'For how long? What's the plan? You do have a

plan, right?'

'Of course.'

Morgan grunts. 'Yeah, of course you do. We're in a stolen Foundation ship complete with a room of kidnapped doctors. You know, there will be quite a few angry people coming after us.'

'I know that, Morgan. We'll deal with the aftermath of taking *Alpha* when we have reinforcements on our side.'

'And the doctors?'

Bray shrugs. 'They know a hell of a lot about the cyborg program. We'd be crazy not to use them.'

Morgan shakes his head and looks back at his daughter. 'You may have a hard time convincing them to cooperate.'

'They'll cooperate, believe me.' Bray rubs his forehead. 'At the moment, the priority is Erin. We need to get her seen to and take some time to figure this out.'

Morgan glances over at him. 'Doesn't sound like much of a plan.'

'It's all I have at the moment. Trust me. I'll figure something out.' Bray checks the coordinates. 'This is it,' he announces.

Morgan frowns at the dilapidated wreck of a station in front of them. 'You sure this is the right place?'

Bray smiles. 'Appearances can be deceiving. It's state of the art inside.'

'Is it big enough to hold *Alpha*?'

'Cronus.'

'Excuse me?'

'*Alpha* is a Foundation designation. I think Cronus suits her better.'

Morgan grunts and shrugs. 'Whatever you say. I'm not up to date with the protocol for renaming a ship after you steal it.' Morgan frowns at the station drifting in front of them. 'Your friends have lived out here for decades?'

Bray nods. 'They're good people. A lot of what they… acquire, from the Foundation goes to the Outer Sector, especially the border worlds.'

'Are you sure Erin will be safe here?'

'I'm sure.'

Morgan doesn't reply and Bray can't blame him. Erin and Morgan have just lost their livelihood, their home, and their freedom if the Foundation ever gets their hands on them. Asking for trust at this stage might be a bit much. He rubs the corner of his eye, but it only makes the pain worse. Once things settle down with his family he'll need to figure out what's going on with his implants. He's not jumping for joy at whatever is happening to his eye.

If anyone can help with that issue too, it's the Dixon's. They should be able to help decipher some of what is on the Foundation systems. If not, they may have to call in help from the Outer Sector. He'd love to bring Cronus back, but until he learns how to pilot her properly, and they find a crew, they're stuck here.

He wipes a trickle of blood from the corner of his

eye trying to clear his vision. There has to be something on the system to explain what's going on with him. Maybe even something to fix Gryffin too.

Something good has to come out of losing Garvan. He meant what he said to Erin. He will figure out a way to go back and get Garvan out. Even if it means bringing the whole Hunter and Nomad fleet back to Earth to help—Gryffin included.

He smiles to himself as they approach the old station. He never thought he'd admit it to himself, but he'd really like to take down the Foundation with Gryffin at his side. It's only right. The Foundation destroyed their lives. The brothers deserve payback for that.

He opens a channel to contact the station. After hearing what Gryffin did to the Scientist on the new colony, he's sure his brother will enjoy tearing the Council apart limb from limb, slowly and painfully.

If you enjoyed *Perses*, please leave a review and tell somebody about the book. Reviews and shares are always welcome.

Thanks for your support!

The adventure continues in

CRONUS

Due 2021

Read on for an excerpt...

CRONUS

Roman shuts down the comms channel and leans back in his chair. He takes a deep breath and swivels around to face Chayse. 'Is the message legit?'

Chayse nods. 'Checked it four times. Not sure how Bray did it, but the signal was bounced through the Port with a Foundation ship. It was sent a few days ago.'

Roman rises to his feet and paces the comms room, ignoring the strange looks from the other occupants. 'It is worth the risk? I mean, I know you and Milla have done everything you can for Gryffin and the others, but could we really decipher the information? Is there a possibility the work to Gryffin can be undone?'

Chayse frowns. 'I haven't got a clue what to say?' He looks over at the blank screen and thinks for a moment. 'To be honest, yes, I think it can. Obviously, we'd have to check the data in more detail, if we can access it, but if Bray thinks it's a good idea, then it must be. He knows more about the Foundation work than any of us here—Avoca made sure of that.'

'I never thought there'd be a way of undoing what

Callum did.'

Chayse holds up a hand. 'Don't get carried away. Bray isn't saying that. There's a possibility some of it can be undone—definitely not all, but you're right. It's a hell of a lot better than surviving the way he is now.'

'Okay, so let's just say we agree this is his best option, how do you think he'll react?'

Chayse makes a face. 'Badly. Going to Earth isn't even on the bottom of his to-do-list. I fully believe, as his father, you should do the honours.' Chayse quickly gets to his feet and hurries away before Roman can object.

Roman sighs, runs a hand over his cropped hair and looks at the door. With no other reason to delay and with no last minute crisis to deal with, Roman decides to get it over with.

This isn't a conversation he's looking forward to. Even through Gryffin is seriously unwell, the thought of going anywhere near Earth doesn't sit well with Roman, let alone Gryffin. His son has been through enough procedures without shipping him to Foundation space for more. Having the information from the Council is a definite bonus though. When Bray and Garvan disappeared along with *Alpha*, a bit of Roman thought that would be the last anyone heard from them. It says a great deal about the men that they survived a stay on Foundation Earth and even managed to take the Council's pride and joy. He smiles to himself. He really wishes he could see the

Council's faces when they realised their ship had been taken by Outer Sector rebels.

'Sir, everything all right?'

Roman jumps slightly and looks at the security guard. He must have walked to the cells on autopilot. 'Of course. Is he alone?'

The security guard makes a face. 'Are you seriously asking me that?'

Roman smiles. 'Terra, right.'

'As always. She's been here for about two hours. I heard Gryffin tell her to leave, but she was equally as forceful when she refused.'

'Thank you. We'll be fine for a few minutes, if you want a break.' Taking the hint, the guard salutes and saunters down the corridor, whistling to himself. Roman holds out his hand to the door, takes a deep breath and places his palm on the lock.

As usual, Terra is working on the small desk against the far wall. Ship and base reports are neatly piled on the floor around the desk. Instead of having her head buried in a report, he's relieved to see her drawing.

Completely engrossed in her drawing, she doesn't notice him come in. Every few seconds she glances up at Gryffin, then back at her pad. Dark pencil blackens the tips of her fingers as she rubs and blurs the lines, softening the pencil marks. Terra never liked drawing on a unit. When it came to her art, she was very old fashioned. Pencils and paper were her only tools. Luckily, Ultar has plenty of both, more than enough to keep her supplied for many years.

He looks over at his son, wondering what she could be focusing her drawing on. The image facing him is not something he'd want to immortalise in a drawing. Gryffin seems to be asleep, but his rest is far from soothing. His metal arm twitches and small sparks of electricity race across the surface. The metal brace supporting his leg rattles against the bars as he shifts on the small cot. His hair and pale face is wet with sweat. The black t-shirt has ridden up, exposing the ribs standing out from his chest. The rare times he's been interested in eating usually ends with the food making a reappearance. Milla was reduced to giving him supplements or injections, anything to help get some nutrients in to him.

His implants weren't faring any better than his biological body. This robotic eye shut down a few days ago and the other is less than reliable, the headache is a constant and nothing Milla does offers any relief. His arm still works, but like his remaining eye, it is intermittent at best. It's his leg that is giving Milla and Chayse the most problems. Nothing they try makes it any better. The last update he had from them this morning ended with the mention of amputation. It is something Gryffin is dead against, but it is getting to the stage where it is lose his leg or his life.

This lifeline from Bray couldn't have come at a better time. Now all he has to do is convince Gryffin to take hold of it.

'How long have you been there?'

He smiles at Terra and shrugs. 'A few minutes. How is he?'

'No worse. He's been asleep for about an hour.' Her tone is cheery, but Roman can see the worry etched around her eyes.

'Speaking of sleep—'

'I had five hours last night. I'm fine, really.'

Gryffin groans in his sleep and Terra instantly gets to her feet. Gryffin's brow furrows and he buries his head under his flesh arm, grabbing onto his hair as he thrashes in the bed. Terra shouts out to him, calling his name over and over until he eventually stills and sits up suddenly. He looks around the room, then from Roman to Terra.

'Hey, you okay?' Terra asks.

He nods once and runs a hand through his damp hair as he takes a deep breath. 'Yeah. I thought I told you to leave?'

'Stop wasting your breath. You need anything?'

He shakes his head and slowly pulls himself up the bed to lean against the back wall.

Roman looks away from his son. He looks even worse awake than he did asleep. 'I have some news. We just got a message from Bray.'

That instantly gets Gryffin and Terra's attention. 'Is he okay?' Terra asks.

'Seems to be. He's hiding out with some friends of Avoca's. *Perses* and *Lir* have just entered the system. It was only a short message, piggybacked on a

Foundation cruiser as it came through the Port. He was able to... steal *Alpha*.'

Gryffin stares at him as he shuffles down the bed. 'Say that again?'

'He's got *Alpha*. He's also got the Foundation's cyborg lab and all of the data. The Council relocated everything to *Alpha* thinking it would be safe there.' Roman laughs and shakes his head. 'Guess they didn't count on Bray doing something completely stupid.'

Terra smiles as she looks up at Roman. 'Does that mean Milla could fix Gryffin?'

Roman shrugs. 'We need to get to the data and unlock it first. We're a long way from knowing what exactly we have access to.'

Her smiles only grows. 'But it's a good start, right?'

Roman nods as he looks away from the hope in her eyes. Having access to the information is one thing. Using it to fix Gryffin before he... well, that's completely different.

Gryffin grunts as he manoeuvres his damaged leg. 'There's a catch, right.'

Roman nods at Gryffin. 'There's no way to get *Alpha* here at the moment. She needs a full crew to operate anything but her drive engines. It would take months to get her here in drive. So, we either send a crew there to spend the next few weeks learning how she works, or... '

Gryffin's eye narrows. 'Hell no.'

Roman sits on the stool by the bars and clasps his hands on his knees. 'I know it's not ideal—'

Gryffin's lifeless robotic eye stares unblinking at him. 'That's an understatement. I'm not going to Earth.'

Terra tries to take his hand through the bars but he pulls it out of the way. 'Gryffin—'

'Don't, Terra. I'd prefer to rot in here than go anywhere near that planet.'

The smile that was on Terra's face a few minutes ago disappears. 'Now you're just being ridiculous. The equipment on *Alpha* could save your life. Are you really that stubborn you'd sacrifice yourself because of your damn pride?'

His face hardens as he meets her eyes. 'Yes.'

She shakes her head and pushes to her feet. Terra paces the far side of the room, trying to get her temper under control. Roman takes a deep breath before he tries again. 'The people Bray is with are trustworthy.'

'You know them?'

Roman makes a face. 'Not personally, no.'

'How do you know they don't work for the Foundation? I'm not keen on being finished. If I go there with the rest of the cyborgs from Ultar, we could be handing the Foundation the start of their army.'

Terra spins to face him, one hand on her hip as she glares at him. 'And if you stay here you will all die. Do you understand that? How about we ask the others what they want to do? This is an important decision, you shouldn't be making it for them.'

'Get the hell out of here.'

Roman opens his mouth to reply but Gryffin's lone eye targets him, cutting off any words that might have been tempted to leave his mouth. He nods to Terra who, after glaring at Gryffin, follows him from the room. She slams the door shut and kicks it for good measure.

'I could just...' she mimes strangling someone then shouts and kicks the door again.

Roman places a hand on her shoulder. 'Hey, you know what he's like.'

'Yeah. Stubborn, irritating, and did I mention stubborn?'

Roman smiles. 'Give him time. It's asking a lot.'

'We don't have time.' Terra gestures angrily at the door. 'We're trying to save his life. I don't get him. A few days ago, he told me he wants to live. He actually said the words. How can he get what he wants but still refuse to cooperate? I swear I'm going to go insane trying to figure him out.'

'We have to see it from his side. He doesn't have a lot of good memories of the Foundation. It's understandable he would be less than keen about going to Foundation space to a commandeered Foundation ship to be worked on with Foundation equipment... again.' He leads her away from the cell and back down the corridor. 'Perhaps a bit of thinking time for all of us would be a good thing.'

Terra glances over her shoulder at the door. 'Probably a good idea. In my current mood, I could very easily…' she lets the sentence go unfinished, but Roman has no doubts she'd like to beat some sense into his son, and he can't blame her. Without a miracle, Gryffin won't be around for much longer.

∞

Sayber looks out the window at the large station in front of them. 'Readings?'

'Nothing, sir,' Quinn reports. 'As far as I can tell it's a hunk of scrap metal.'

Sayber turns to face Avoca. 'You sure about this?'

Avoca nods. 'Readings can be deceptive. Trust me, this is the right place.'

Sayber examines the floating wreck again. 'How can you be so sure your mates won't run straight to the Foundation as soon as we make contact?'

'Not everyone in this Sector follows the rule of the Foundation. These people have opposed the Council for as long as I've known them. We'll be safe here.'

Sayber leans over Quinn's shoulder and checks the readings again. He's stalling but it's not a decision he wants to rush in to. Putting his faith, his crew, and his ship in the hands of a Foundation admiral goes against everything he is, but he's not stupid or proud enough to dismiss Avoca's help. He's out of his depth in this Sector. 'Don't have much choice I guess.'

Avoca squeezes his shoulder briefly then nods at

Quinn. 'Uncloak and bring us a little closer. Ask *Lir* to do the same.'

Quinn glances at Sayber for confirmation. Sayber pauses for a few seconds then nods once. Quinn relays the message to Rua as he guides *Perses* towards the station. 'We're being contacted, sir.' Quinn frowns as he reads the message on the screen.

'What is it?'

'Either the system is screwed up or there's someone just as screwed up over there. It just says, "JAM." That's it.'

Sayber glares over his shoulder at Avoca as the man laughs. 'He's screwed up all right. Reply with - PLUM.'

Quinn looks to Sayber for help but his captain just shrugs. 'Do what he says.'

Quinn takes a deep breath then relays the message to the station. 'Sir, the cargo doors are opening. Still no power readings coming from the station. I don't understand.'

'You and me both. Avoca?'

The Admiral nods towards the station. 'I suggest we get in there before someone sees us.'

'What the hell. We're sitting targets out here. Take us in.' Sayber leaves Quinn to guide *Perses* in and lowers into his chair again. 'Who are these people?'

Avoca leans against the console behind him. 'Evie and Felix Dixon. They lived next door to me and my family for years. They both dutifully followed the Foundation ideals for...' he blows out a breath, 'it must be about fifty years or so. Then one day, they decided they'd had enough. They vanished from the Foundation system. About two years after they vanished, they contacted me again. They knew I felt as disillusioned about the Foundation as they did so felt they could trust me. The first time I came here I was amazed. They had managed to build a life out here completely off the grid. They used their saved credits to transform this place. They've built up a network of black market traders, and supply the border worlds with whatever they need.'

Sayber whistles. 'Impressive.' Anything else he is going to say is cut off as *Perses* enters the station. Lights guide the ships towards a large landing platform. About a dozen transports of various different sizes, condition, and age line the far side of the platform but it's the mammoth vessel to the back of the station that gets his attention. He's never seen something so big. The enormous Foundation symbol plastered on her hull gives him reason to pause.

'I don't like the look of this. Why is there a Foundation ship here?'

'Whatever the reason the Dixon's would not betray us.' Avoca slaps Sayber on the back. 'Just follow my lead.'

'Yeah, sure. Quinn, stay here. If anything looks off, get *Perses* out of here. Got it?'

'Yes, sir.'

Sayber walks with Avoca to the cargo hold and tries to steady his nerves as the back lowers. He steps onto the ramp and looks around him. He nods at Rua as the captain pauses at the base of *Lir*'s ramp to his left. Both captains examine the inside of the station. The derelict station deception is effective. From the outside you would never guess at what is really going on inside. State of the art atmospheric units circulate fresh, cool air around the cargo hold. A team busily works on a platform to his right, unloading crates stamped with the Foundation logo from a transport. Sayber smirks. He likes these people already.

Two double height doors ahead of them burst slide open and a couple walks out. Evie and Felix Dixon couldn't be further from what Sayber had envisioned. After only spending a few minutes on the station and seeing a small part of the operation, Sayber had pictured an imposing couple. The truth is a far different picture. Dressed in a red blazer, white shirt, green cargo shorts and black boots, Felix doesn't fit his surroundings. Evie follows after him in a knee length skirt, heavy navy jumper and brown sandals. Her greying wiry hair is stuffed under a wide brimmed hat with a large flower sticking out of it. 'Different.'

Avoca smiles and laughs. 'They prefer eclectic.'

Felix waves his arm at the security. 'Get out of my way. Move!'

The men step aside, giving the couple room to pass. 'Well, well, well. Think I may finally be losing it. Hank Avoca?'

'You're looking well, Felix. Evie, you haven't aged.'

'And you're still a lousy liar, Hank.' She smiles and embraces him.

'No hugging yet,' Felix interrupts. 'Payment first.'

Sayber tenses at the comment, but Avoca merely nods and walks back up the ramp. He unfastens one of the crates he brought from Ultar and takes something out. He passes it to Felix who takes it from Avoca as if it was pure gold. 'Plum jam.'

'What?' Sayber asks.

Felix glances at Sayber. 'Plum jam.' He repeats each word slowly. 'Did you get it that time?' Felix looks at Avoca. 'What's his problem?'

Sayber grinds his teeth as the two men laugh at him. 'You brought a crate of jam from Ultar? I told you to pack essentials.'

'And I did. I thought we might be needing some help. The Dixon's are partial to plum jam.'

'Can't get it out here. Plums are reserved for the elite Foundation fat-cats.' Felix gestures behind him. 'Unload it. If even one jar goes missing, heads will roll. Now, dinner is just about ready. Can I presume there are more than just the three of you on these ships?'

Avoca nods. 'There's a full crew on each.'

Evie steps closer to Rua. 'Apologies, we've been ignoring you. Rogue?'

Rua nods. 'That a problem?'

Evie laughs. 'Heaven's no. You the only woman?'

Rua shakes her head. 'My crew is all female.'

Evie squeals and claps her hand. 'You've made my

day, Captain. It's a little testosterone heavy around here.' She waves her hand at the group of men standing beside Felix. 'Hey, you with the gun.'

'They've all got guns,' Felix responds.

'That one there. What's his name?'

Felix shrugs. 'How am I expected to remember?'

'You hired them all.'

'Yeah, but they look the same. Big men with guns.'

She nudges Rua in the side. 'The small ones didn't work.' She leans closer. 'Can you imagine having a protection detail full of men that looked like Felix. He couldn't scare a fly off a corpse.' She waves at the man beside Felix again. Something about his stance tells Sayber he's the leader of the protection detail. Dressed in black combats and a green t-shirt, the tall, broad, menacing looking man with short, dark brown hair takes a step forward. 'Yes, you. Big guy, would you be a dear and make sure we've got enough room in the mess for the crew.'

The man sighs as he walks over to Evie. 'It's Heath.'

She pats him on his arm. 'Whatever you say.' She turns to Rua. 'He's been keeping us safe for years now. He's a big softy really, well, unless you get on his wrong side.' She leans closer and lowers her voice. 'Saw him kill someone with his bare hands once. Best security in the Sector. Isn't that right, fellow.'

He groans as he gestures to the rest of his men standing beside Felix. 'And you still don't know my name.'

'What was that, dear?' Evie asks.

'Nothing.' He addresses Rua and Sayber, 'Unload your people. After you eat, we can have a look at your ships, see if anything needs to be done.'

Rua looks over at Sayber and he shrugs. 'I'm game if you are.' Rua turns her attention back to Heath and quietly examines him.

Heath holsters his gun and holds his hands out. 'I get why you're wary, but Hank is a friend of the Dixon's. We got your backs while you're here.'

The door behind them slides aside again and a familiar face walks out. Bray smiles at Sayber as he approaches his captain. He stands in front of Sayber and salutes. 'I can't believe you're here.'

Sayber smiles. 'Couldn't have you going AWOL on me. If I needed to come here personally and drag you back, so be it.' He gestures over his shoulder at the hulking form of *Alpha* behind him. 'Should I ask?'

Bray grins as he proudly looks at the ship. 'I didn't think the Foundation deserved her.' He shrugs. 'You never know, she might come in handy.'

'You don't say.' Sayber looks around the group of mismatched people. 'Where's your mate?'

Bray's face drops. 'Still on Earth. It's a long story. Fill you in over dinner?'

'Sounds good.'

Bray looks over Sayber's shoulder at Rua, standing on the loading ramp of *Lir*. 'Captain.'

A whisper of a smile crosses her lips before it disappears. She nods at him then turns to the Rogue beside her. 'Regan, assemble the crew. I want a team on board at all times. Take it in shifts.'

Seeing that everyone is in agreement, Evie claps her hands together. 'Fantastic. Time for dinner.'

'Couldn't agree more,' Felix says. 'My stomach feels like my throat's been cut.'

'Oh you're always hungry. Don't think I won't be keeping an eye on those jam jars too. I know what you're like. I haven't forgotten about the cake.'

'Seriously, woman. Can you not let that go? We have company.'

She thumps him full force in the arm. 'Do not call me woman, and no, I will not let it go. It was my birthday cake.'

'And it was delicious.'

Evie glowers at her husband for a moment, then turns away from him with a snort. 'Big fellow, I'll leave you to organise the people.'

Heath closes his eyes and curses under his breath. 'I swear she does it on purpose.' He steps away to speak to his team while Avoca, Sayber, Bray and Rua follow the Dixon's through the large doors.

Sayber and Rua fall into step beside Avoca. 'They always like this?' Rua asks.

Avoca nods. 'Don't let them fool you. Heath and his men are the muscle, but the Dixon's are, without a doubt, the brains behind this station. Anything they don't know about smuggling, hacking systems, or evading detection isn't worth knowing.'

'You're putting a lot of faith in them,' Rua says.

'They haven't let me down in the past.'

Sayber stops Avoca. 'You've used them before?'

'Of course.'

'Why would an upstanding Foundation admiral need smugglers?'

'How do you think I got Bray out of Tyrat?' Avoca puts his hand on Bray's shoulder. 'They organised everything for me.'

Bray leads them down the corridor and into a large open plan mess. 'I spent a few weeks here recovering from Tyrat. They're good people.'

'Will they be able to help with Garvan and Gryffin?'

Bray takes a deep breath before answering Sayber. 'I hope so, for all our sakes.'

ARES

NOMAD SERIES BOOK 1
(available as paperback, ebook and audio)

He wasn't expected to survive. No one else did, and for twenty years, he has managed to stay off their radar. Until now. Until her.

Gryffin was the sole survivor of The Foundation's experimental project to transform human children into hybrid cyborgs - half human, half machine. The program failed and he was sent on a one way trip into The Outer Sector where he was left for dead. He has survived for twenty years by suppressing his human emotions and embracing his machine side.

Officer Terra Rush believes in her duty to the Foundation. The Sector needs to be prepared for colonization, and nothing can stop her from doing her job...except him. When Gryffin saves her from an attack, Terra uncovers a terrible secret. The Foundation has been lying to her...and maybe they still are.

They have labelled Gryffin a killing machine, yet he acts more human than many of The Foundation's leaders. He has awakened intense feelings in Terra that throw her loyalties into question, and even though he pushes her away, she is determined to find out the truth about the cyborg program.

Gryffin refuses to be a mindless soldier, yet escaping The Foundation's control and stopping the colonization of his home will require Terra's help. Can Gryffin overcome the machine inside and trust her? Or will getting in touch with his human emotions destroy him once and for all?

NEMESIS

NOMAD SERIES BOOK 2

(available as paperback, ebook and audio)

A part of her died when she lost him.

Commander Terra Rush has spent the last eight months mourning Gryffin, believing he died when his ship crashed. When he returns to her, broken and scarred from months of torture at the hands of the Foundation, it feels like a miracle - at first.

His unpredictable mechanical side, reawakened by the brutality he endured as a prisoner, threatens to destroy him. He's lost the trust of the colonists. Has he lost part of himself as well?

Her need to protect her ravaged heart puts distance between them when they need to depend on each other the most. If the colonists are to survive, they need Gryffin to reunite the Nomad and stand with them...and he needs Terra's help to do so. But time and tragedy have changed them both so much. Can they find their way back to each other before everything they know is destroyed?